ROYAL BASTARDS MC

TONOPAH, NV

D1563593

USA Today Bestselling Author

NIKKI LANDIS

Copyright © 2022 Nikki Landis

All Rights Reserved.

ISBN 9798846695146

No part of this publication may be reproduced, distributed, or transmitted in any form or by any means, including photocopying, recording, or other electronic or mechanical methods, without the prior written permission of the publisher, except in the case of brief quotations embodied in critical reviews and certain other noncommercial uses permitted by copyright law.

This is a work of fiction. Names, places, and incidents are products of the author's imagination or are used fictitiously and are not to be construed as real. Any resemblance to actual events, locales, organizations, or persons, living or dead, is entirely coincidental.

Cover by Syn Ink LLC

Table of Contents

AUTHOR'S NOTE

Twitchy's story began in the Royal Harlots MC Anthology, part of the Royal Bastards MC world. This book is a Royal Bastards MC/Royal Harlots MC crossover combining both Twitchy and Ace's stories.

The events in *Violent Bones* take place during the same time frame as *Eternally Mine* and before *Twisted Devil*. It's highly recommended to read the series in order, especially *Devil's Ride*, *Hell's Fury*, and *Eternally Mine*. There's much more to come from Grim and his Reapers. Be sure to follow me on social media and be the first to learn of each new release!

ROYAL BASTARDS MC

ROYAL BASTARDS CODE

PROTECT: The club and your brothers come before anything else, and must be protected at all costs. **CLUB** is **FAMILY**.

RESPECT: Earn it & Give it. Respect club law. Respect the patch. Respect your brothers. Disrespect a member and there will be hell to pay.

HONOR: Being patched in is an honor, not a right. Your colors are sacred, not to be left alone, and **NEVER** let them touch the ground.

OL' LADIES: Never disrespect a member's or brother's Ol' Lady. **PERIOD.**

CHURCH is **MANDATORY.**

LOYALTY: Takes precedence over all, including well-being.

HONESTY: Never **LIE, CHEAT,** or **STEAL** from another member or the club.

TERRITORY: You are to respect your brother's property and follow their Chapter's club rules.

TRUST: Years to earn it...seconds to lose it.
NEVER RIDE OFF: Brothers do not abandon their family.

COMMON TERMS

Reaper demonic entity sharing the body of every Royal Bastard club member in the Tonopah chapter

Devil's Ride a deadly motorcycle ride into the Nevada desert and initiation into the club

Cage vehicle

Hog motorcycle

Pres president of the club

SAA Sargeant at Arms

Ol' lady a member's property, his woman, respected and cherished

Cut leather jacket with the sleeves cut off, member patches on the front and club logo on the back, sacred to members

Church an official club meeting

Chapel the location for church meetings in the Crossroads

Crossroads RBMC Tonopah Chapter clubhouse

Prospect someone interested in patching with the club, sponsored by a member

Muffler bunny club girl, also called sweet butt, cut slut

Bloody Scorpions BSMC, rival motorcycle club

Black Market Railroad Human trafficking ring, connections to Russian bratva

Royal Bastards MC

Tonopah, NV

Bones:

Violence is a normal part of my life.

I've lived it, one way or another, since the day I enlisted.

In the Corps, they called me Ace.

A sharpshooter, I never missed.

But after I retired, I felt restless, searching for meaning until I found Hope's Refuge.

Mercy took a chance on a cocky Marine.

I found my purpose in handing out justice and helping women and children in need.

So when Mercy asked me to follow his daughter and keep her safe, I thought the job would be easy.

Until I saw her.

Davina is a goddess. The perfect woman. Trouble disguised with a confident, sensual smile.

Getting close to her just might be my downfall.

Not one enemy overseas could take me down, but this feisty Harlot has me locked down and begging for more.

Can I resist falling for her and keep my focus on her safety?

Twitchy:

I've always been independent. Tough. Lethal.

My daddy didn't raise a weak woman.

I learned to shoot a gun at twelve and fight in the ring with my brother at thirteen.

Relationships and love aren't in the cards for me.

I'm too damn picky, and I don't like to be controlled.

I guess you could say I'm a dominant personality.

I've got it all figured out until I meet Ace.

He's a tattooed, imposing, dark warrior who makes me want to act on all the fantasies in my head.

He's charming, loyal, and deadly.

This Marine knows how to take charge and gives as good as he gets.

I don't want to fall in love. I swear he's just a fling.

And then my stupid heart starts calling the shots, complicating things between us.

When my life is on the line, I can't help thinking of Ace first.

Can he save me from my enemies before it's too late?

PLAYLIST

Shadows – Blasterjaxx & Hollywood Undead

Kill Beautiful Things – DED

Mayhem – Halestorm

Sweet but Psycho – Ava Max

Enemy – Imagine Dragons, JID & League of Legends

Eye of the Storm – Pop Evil

Anti-Everything – DED

Trouble – JJ Wilde

Eternally Yours – Motionless In White

Black Sheep – Dorothy

Runaway – Hollywood Undead & Imanbek

River – Bishop Briggs

Bones – Imagine Dragons

Something in the Orange – Zach Bryan

Faster – Within Temptation

Heart of a Champion (feat. Papa Roach & Ice Nine Kills) – Hollywood Undead

The Drug in Me Is Reimagined – Falling In Reverse

Colossus – Avatar

A Conversation with Death – Khemmis

Talking Body – Tove Lo

You can listen to Nikki's playlists on Spotify.

ROYAL BASTARDS MC

ONE

Twitchy

T HE WIND HOWLED AND shook the cable lines outside the Coroner's Office as I shivered, glaring at the racket above my head as I knocked on the door. The heavy steel door creaked beneath my fist as I pounded a second time. This wasn't the main entrance everyone else used.

I had my own private entryway into the house of death whenever I wanted, thanks to my friendship with Bludge— short for Bludgeon. Don't ask me why the best slice and dice master in Vegas was given that name. It happened long before we ever met.

A haggard face appeared in the tiny window at the top, and I caught the bloodshot green eyes peeking at me as they narrowed. "What you want this late, Twitch?"

"Fucking hell, Bludge. Let me in. My tits are gonna freeze, and I'll have permanent nipple hard-on for the rest of my days."

There was a snort, and the locks clicked before the burly bastard opened the door and stood back, letting me slip inside. "You got a body or what? It's too fucking cold to go out there twice tonight."

I ticked my head toward the SUV I'd snatched from Grim, the president of the Royal Bastards MC. He'd be pissed when he realized I didn't ask for permission, but I left my bike at their compound, so I figured it was a fair trade until I returned to the Crossroads. "In the back."

He gave a brisk nod and then charged toward the vehicle, opening the back hatch and snatching up the poor girl I wrapped up in a stolen motel sheet.

Damn. I sure lived a morbid life.

He managed to snap the back shut and rush inside with the body, trudging down the hall to his lab. I shut the door behind him and turned the locks, ensuring we wouldn't be disturbed.

"Where did you find this one?" Bludge was already carefully unwrapping her, assessing the woman's body for injuries and cause of death so quickly that I knew he would have answers for me faster than I could have ever obtained on my own. He was the best when it came to identification. It didn't hurt that the guy I relied on most when I needed help in these kinds of circumstances was also Tonopah's coroner.

"In Stefanie Holloway's grave."

This girl, whoever she was, deserved to be buried properly. Her family needed the closure. Guilt for not dropping her off to the police sooner seized my gut and I winced but this was too important to ignore. I had to learn the details about her first. If I had any hope of stopping those Russian traffickers from kidnapping more girls, I needed answers.

Only one place provided the discretion I needed. One man who could give me the answers I needed. That was why I came here.

He whistled low, shaking his head.

"No shit? The girl that went missing four months ago?"

"Yep. I had to do a little digging, but this isn't Stefanie."

He snorted at the double meaning. "Right."

Just thinking of Shadow and the reunion between the young couple was enough to make my black heart happy. Never met a guy so in love with his girl or willing to die for her the way Shadow had been for Stefanie. Maybe someday I'd meet someone who wanted me with that level of conviction. Until then, I'd be happy to ride whatever cock I wanted and leave when I finished.

"We won't know if it's Stefanie until I plug the DNA into all the databases," he contradicted, snipping off the eroded clothes and carefully separating the jewelry and other items from the corpse. I'd clean and package them for the family once Bludge cataloged the details.

"Well, I think I know the answer to that. We just rescued Stefanie from a human trafficking ring."

His gaze shot up from where he'd been perusing the bones, locking on my face with a frown. "Fucking hell."

"Yeah. Russians, Scorpions MC, and a whole lot of trouble."

"This Harlots business or Royal Bastards?" Bludge resumed his study of the body, documenting information and injuries as well as defining the cause of death.

"Is there ever a time when they don't overlap?" I asked, slightly sarcastic.

"Don't get all twisted around me, Twitchy. We've done this song and dance too long to fool one another."

"I know," I admitted, rubbing my eyes. "I've been up for two fucking days. I need to rest."

"Got that room in the back. Always available. You know that."

"I know."

"You got someplace else to be right now?"

"No, not until tomorrow afternoon," I admitted.

"Then go rest for a few hours. When you wake up, I'll be finished. You owe me breakfast."

Slapping him on the shoulder, I laughed. "I'll take care of you." Lifting on my tiptoes, I pressed a kiss to his cheek. "Thanks, Bludge."

He grumbled a reply as I dragged my weary ass across the room and down the sterile, clean hall toward the only space I could get rest for the foreseeable future. Life was finding a way to catch up with me faster than I could run. At this rate, I'd never fulfill the promise I made, and that was unacceptable.

Just a few hours—that was all I needed.

The rest of the shit could wait.

SOMETHING POUNDED HARD ON the side of my skull as I mumbled in my sleep, rolling over to tug the pillow tighter over my head. *Shit.* It wasn't my head taking the beating but the fucking door.

I'd always been a grump about my rest, and I hated being awakened early. A few curses left my lips as I tried to drown out the loud, obnoxious noises coming from beyond the room, which was supposed to be my temporary sanctuary. My eyes were nearly sealed shut by my mascara, and it took a minute before I could check the time on my phone.

Four lousy hours.

That was all the sleep I'd gotten, thanks to the inconsiderate person still slamming their fist into the door, demanding to be let inside the morgue. By now, I could hear the guy yelling and threatening Bludge with bodily harm. Rising off the mattress, I picked up my gun and marched across the cold floors, flinging open my door before I stomped down the corridor to the side entrance I had used earlier. Whoever lingered outside knew to use the private entry. The outer door groaned in protest with every fist that hit the surface.

Flinging it open, I cocked my gun and pointed it at the asshole who dared to wake me up with this ruckus. "What the fuck do you want?"

If he was surprised to find a half-naked woman open the door to the morgue, he didn't show it.

"Damn, sweetness. You can't answer the door like that. It's not safe."

I stared the guy down, annoyed that he was attractive in all the ways I found addicting—broad, sculpted shoulders, scruff a few days old on his angular, handsome face, hypnotic blue eyes, and that cocky stance that proved he liked trouble and thrived on it. His military haircut confirmed he was disciplined and knew his way around firearms, further increasing my interest.

Mr. Sexy-as-fuck-bedroom-eyes stared me down, briefly blinking as he took in my appearance, a devilish smile twisting his lips. There was no denying the fact that he was checking me out. Pretty damn sure he enjoyed seeing my black thong and the little the fabric did to conceal my girly bits.

"Is there a reason you're pounding on the door and interrupting my beauty sleep? It's four in the morning."

"Apologies for waking you, beautiful. Had I known, I would have been prepared for the goddess standing on the other side of the door."

Right.

"Flattery doesn't work on me," I snarled, annoyed but also curious about this clean-cut military man and his too-wide shoulders.

"That's a shame, sweetheart. I think you must have dated the wrong men."

"I'm tempted to tell you that I'm a lesbian, so you'll back off, but the truth is I like cock far too much to joke around about it."

He blinked twice, slightly taken aback, before a slow, seductive smile curved the edges of his lips. "Where have you been all my life, gorgeous?"

"Trying to sleep," I deadpanned, highly annoyed with his pretty-boy grin and rippling muscles.

"I can solve your problem. You just need to be tired enough." He flashed a wolfish smile and then charged forward, wrapping an arm around my waist and shoving his way inside.

In two seconds flat, I was pressed against the door, caged beneath his powerful body. My right hand clenched the gun, but his palm covered the weapon, holding the barrel still and rendering it useless. Thick thighs surrounded my hips on either side as he leaned down, searching my eyes for answers I'd never divulge.

"You sure are hellfire, kitten. Exactly the kind of burn I like." His nostrils flared as I shoved at his chest with my free hand, failing to budge him an inch. "But we got a problem, goddess. I need to talk to Bludge. He's the only one who can help me."

"What's your name?" I asked, ignoring the heat of his body and the impulse to snuggle closer since he drove away the chill lingering in the air.

"Ace."

Tilting my head slightly, I tried to make sense of the man who didn't seem to be in a hurry to back off. "Just Ace?"

"Just Ace. I never miss my mark. Always a hole in one," he rasped, dropping another inch closer to my lips. "Good thing that's what you like."

Snorting, I wasn't the least bit surprised to find his ego matched his physique. "Release me, or your balls will suffer the consequences." My knee lifted slightly, and he swiveled his hips, driving that thick rod between his legs right up against me. He was sporting some major wood, and I had to focus so I didn't slide my hand down and grip his significant bulge.

"I don't think you want to play that rough, beautiful." His free hand slid down the side of my face, tracing my jawline until it rested on my throat. "Or do you?"

"You done playing with her yet?" Bludge asked in an annoyed tone. "Fuck if you aren't always whipping your dick out for the ladies."

Ace chuckled, backing away as his hungry, predatory gaze slid down the entire length of my body. "This time, I'm not just playin'. I don't want a lick of the lollipop. I want to devour the whole damn sucker."

Bludge belted out a laugh and shook his head. "Stop fucking with Twitchy. She's deadly."

"Oh, I don't doubt it," Ace agreed. "Already stole my heart right from my chest." He winked in my direction before he spun around, reluctantly sweeping his gaze over me one final time.

When he followed Bludge into his office, I stared after him like a girl with her high school crush. *Fucking men.* Sometimes I did wish I didn't love cock so much. I'd save myself a lot of trouble.

ROYAL BASTARDS MC

TWO

Twitchy

"**W**HERE ARE YOU RUNNIN' off to, goddess?"

Ace's raspy, deep voice seemed to carry across the whole damn building.

"Breakfast," I whispered, placing a finger over my lips. "I promised Bludge. Don't wake him."

"I'll come with you. Need coffee ASAP, honey. The shit he's brewin' isn't much better than motor oil, and there wasn't a goddamn thing in his fridge but body parts and blood."

That was why I wouldn't drink Bludge's coffee or touch anything in the morgue.

"Better hurry up. I don't wait for anyone." Pulling my keys from my pocket, I led the way outdoors and into the bright sunshine streaming over the horizon like spilled, amber-colored buttermilk. Everything in the vicinity was painted with a pale, shimmering glow.

Pretty as a new peach, as my Mama used to say.

Ace didn't bother reaching for my keys, and I liked how he swaggered confidently to the passenger door, sliding inside the front seat once I hit the fob. Most guys I dated were macho, glory-hogging chauvinists who didn't like to give up control. Ace wasn't bothered in the least.

Damn, if that wasn't as attractive as a shiny new pistol.

We drove to the local diner and ordered food to go as the waitress offered us both coffees. Ace took his black, but I had to add a dash of cream and a couple of sugars.

"Thanks," I replied as I took the cup and slipped one of the corrugated sleeves over the piping hot exterior. My ass landed on one of the stools at the counter as I sipped on my caffeine and chanced a glance in Ace's direction. He was staring at me as if no one else in the restaurant existed.

"You keep lookin' at me like I'm the tastiest snack you ever met, and I might start to think you want more than a one-night stand."

"Already told you, gorgeous. I'm in this for the long haul."

Snorting, I winked in his direction. "You don't need to play games with me. If I want to fuck you, we'll fuck. If not, we won't. Not interested in any kind of relationship."

Ace frowned, leaning forward as his arm draped across the counter. "You're gonna learn something about me, precious. The bigger the challenge, the harder I chase after it."

"That might work with muffler bunnies, Ace." Leaning closer, I let my free hand caress the side of his jaw down to his chin. "I'm a Royal Harlot. I don't take orders. I don't spread my legs at whim. And I sure as fuck don't let a man control a damn thing I say or do. You're going to be disappointed, heartbroken, or left holding your dick wondering what the fuck happened. That's just how this thing works."

Ace's eyes darkened into deep azure pools, and I wasn't sure if it was desire, the challenge he clearly wanted, or the fact that he was horny as fuck.

I'd bet on all three being correct to some extent.

"Twitchy, baby, you just met your match." There was a hint of something dark and dangerous in Ace's eyes, and fuck me if that wasn't the biggest turn-on yet.

"Breakfast is ready." The waitress plopped a couple of bags full of containers on the counter. "Got all the condiments and silverware. You're all set."

"Thanks, Dina."

"See ya around, Twitchy."

I slapped a couple of twenties on the counter, but Ace shook his head. He picked one up, shoved it into a pocket on the front of my leather jacket, and then dropped two more twenties on the one still lying on the counter.

"Keep the change, Dina."

"Have a good one," she announced, swiping up the money and strolling over to the register.

Ace didn't say much as we returned to the coroner's office. When we arrived, the morgue was shut tight, and I used the spare key Bludge kept in the lab. Once we were back inside, I placed the key back on the little hook above his desk.

"You think he's awake yet?" Ace asked, noting the quiet interior.

"Hell no. Bludge is like a vampire. He works the third shirt. Never see him in the light of day," I admitted with a laugh.

"Then why did you grab breakfast?"

"I'll keep his food in the bag and set it outside his door. Once he's up, he'll reheat everything."

That must have sufficed because Ace nodded. "Well, I'm starving. Let's dig in."

The morgue had a separate employee lounge that Bludge had taken over and turned into a twisted version of a horror movie. There was shit all over, and the mess wasn't the worst part.

Bludge must have been part hoarder because stacks of newspapers, plastic utensils, paper plates, coffee mugs, and creamer cups littered every surface. Boxes of various supplies were open all over the break room, and the sink looked like he'd washed bloody hands but never bothered to wipe it out. Blood dripped down some of the cabinets, and the handles on the fridge were bloody too. It looked like someone had bludgeoned another person to death, and I was sure my favorite slice and dice master appreciated the irony. Funny, this room was such a disaster because the rest of his facility was spotless.

"What the fuck?" Ace blurted, scanning the room with all the blood smears and fingerprints. "This is fucking nasty."

"Haven't you ever been in here before?" I asked, smirking at the look on his face. "I'll eat at the table without blood on it, but that's about it. Bludge is so busy when he's on a case he overlooks the messes he leaves behind, usually just the break room. Trust me; this isn't the worst I've seen."

Ace swiped an arm across one of the tables and sent everything to the floor. "Fuck it. I'll share the damn table, but that's it. I'm not cleaning up after his big hairy ass."

A giggle escaped my throat as I sat across from him and opened the bags, dividing the containers and placing our food on the table. The remainder I put in the bag and tied it shut for Bludge.

"So, how did you meet him?"

Ace shook his head. "It's crazy to think he's so methodical and careful with his job, and yet he's the dirtiest fucker I've ever seen. Been in his private room too. It's as messy as this." Ace shook his head. "Bludge solved an old case for me. Something personal."

Nodding, I didn't ask for specifics. It wasn't my business. "He's good at finding answers and pieces of the puzzle no one else can. Bludge knows bones, and he's got good instincts with anatomy. That's why he's known as the slice and dice man. Best one in the state as far as I know."

"Same. That's why I'm here."

"Well, you won't have to deal with me for long. I just need a few answers," I divulged, digging into my eggs and bacon, along with the English muffin I slathered with apple butter. "He said he'd have them for me before I left."

"Then you're waiting for dusk."

"No. He'll set an alarm and fill me in after he's gotten a few hours of rest. We have a system that works. Bludge never lets me down."

Ace was almost finished with his food already, swiping up gravy and bits of sausage with his biscuit. "I see. What happens when you find those answers that you're looking for?"

Swallowing my food, I chased the bite down with a gulp of coffee. This was as far as I could go in this conversation. Saying anything else placed Ace at risk. Not that I didn't think he couldn't handle himself. I just didn't go against code. This was club business, and Ace wasn't privy to Harlots or Royal Bastards' information. With a shrug, I met his curious gaze. "I react."

"That sounds dangerous, beautiful."

"Life is dangerous."

"Sure is," he agreed, pushing his empty plate aside. "You gonna be alright on your own? No trouble headin' your way?"

Why would he ask that? "You know something I don't, Ace?"

"I don't like the vibe I'm gettin'. Something isn't stirring the Kool-Aid."

Huh? That was the oddest expression I'd ever heard. "Meaning?"

"I don't like the idea of you chasing down death, little firecracker. You got the balls for it—no doubt about that. But shit happens. You can't control everything."

Suddenly feeling uneasy, I leveled him with my most intimidating stare. "Listen, the protective alpha male thing is pretty hot, but I don't like feeling cornered." Whipping out my gun, I cocked the pistol and aimed it at his heart. "Start telling me the parts you're keeping hidden. Who the hell are you, and why the fuck did you show up here? Don't fucking patronize me and say it's got to do with Bludge. You came here for me. Admit it."

"That's the second time you pulled a gun on me, gorgeous. There won't be a third."

"Then answer my questions. It's not my fault my trigger finger tends to get a little twitchy," I snarled, placing my hands together to steady my aim. "I won't miss. Your heart will be shredded in seconds."

He shoved his trash to the side and sat back, crossing his arms. "You're on the Russians' hit list. Black Market Railroad wants you eliminated after all the shit you've pulled. They'll do it too. You're good as dead."

Hiding the fear those words evoked, I inhaled and exhaled, taking that breath nice and slow to steady my nerves. "And you're here to make sure it happens?"

"No, sweetness," he replied gruffly, leaning forward to snatch the barrel of my gun. His long, thick fingers wrapped around the steel as he yanked it from my hand. "I'm here to make sure you don't get killed."

Blinking, I processed the words he said and knew he wasn't a threat. If Ace wanted me dead, he could have done it twenty times already. "Who sent you?" I asked, mildly pissed.

Was it Georgia? Because she never could keep her mouth shut.

Or was it my pres? Because I was a fucking nomad, and I liked it that way. I didn't need everyone up in my business all the damn time.

Staring Ace down, I waited for him to answer, burying the urge to hit something.

"Mercy," he whispered.

All of the air in my lungs left in a *whoosh*. To say I was shocked was an understatement.

"And the Jackal."

Collapsing onto the table, I struggled to breathe as my stomach rested on the chilly surface while I gripped the edges. "Why?"

"I think that's obvious."

"No." My head shook back and forth like a pendulum. "Why did they send *you*?"

Ace placed my gun on a nearby table and then stood, pulling me up against his chest. One finger traced the side of my face as he leaned down, his lips hovering above my own. "Because I volunteered."

"For?"

"Whatever it takes."

"You're speaking in riddles," I accused, growing increasingly frustrated. "Ace—"

His lips crashed down on mine, and I jolted in his embrace, struck like lightning at the passion that radiated from the powerful man who held me as if I was someone he cherished, adored, and couldn't resist one more minute. That didn't make any sense at all.

Then it hit me.

This wasn't the first time Ace saw me. It wasn't possible to feel the way he did when we'd known one another for less than a day. He didn't have to say a word.

I knew all I needed to learn from the way he held me and how that kiss evoked a deep visceral reaction. He groaned as he clutched my body tighter against him, unable to hide the hardness of his dick as the bulge in his pants grew.

Placing my hands on his chest, I pushed, effectively separating us by several inches. "How long?"

"How long what, beautiful?"

"How long have you been spying on me?"

ROYAL BASTARDS MC

THREE

Ace

Six months earlier—

"How LONG HAVE YOU been with us, Ace?" Mercy asked, dropping his bulk into a fat leather chair behind his desk. "Three years?"

"Five, and you know it," I replied with a smirk. "Don't bust my balls."

"Since the day you were discharged. Isn't that right?"

"Yeah. What's this about, Mercy?"

"Got something of a personal nature, and I need someone I can count on. A man I can trust to be discreet and fulfill the job no matter how long it takes."

Sitting back, I folded my arms across my chest. "I'm always here for Hope's Refuge. No questions asked."

"This isn't about Hope's Refuge."

The organization of Hope's Refuge was built many years ago and had connections worldwide. Mercy was good with people—finding them, helping them, saving them. You name it. The man had a knack for locating the lost and broken.

There was something about him that was different. Maybe it was just how he cared for others, especially those who were weak of mind, body, or spirit. They seemed to flock toward him, and he was proficient at providing exactly what they needed.

All free of charge.

His company was funded by donors all over the globe. Powerful men and women that consisted of politicians, actors, artists, musicians, and dignitaries. They believed in the work he did, and that was part of the reason I stuck around. Mercy wasn't in this for the money. He cared about people and was one of few men in power who genuinely didn't have a hidden agenda.

His volunteers were ghosts. Nameless and faceless souls with one task: rescue and help transport victims on their journey to a new home. We had no real identities and used code names for one another. The victims always referred to us as "Ghosts." We never revealed our names or any personal information. All credit was given to Hope's Refuge.

I'd been dubbed Ace for my precision in the Marine Corps and sniper status. Made sense to use the nickname as my Ghost identity. Since the day I arrived, I became one of the busiest Ghosts in Mercy's group. Maybe it was all the time I had on my hands, or perhaps I just volunteered more than the others since I didn't like being idle. Either way, he trusted me with missions not everyone else knew about.

"Then what is it? What do you need?"

"My daughter," he growled, rising to his feet. "She's a Royal Harlot."

Blinking, I had to process this information because I didn't know Mercy had any kids.

Five years I'd worked with him, and this was news I'd never even heard whispers about before now. "Holy shit. You have a kid?"

"Two," a gruff voice announced as the door opened. The tall, imposing figure of the Jackal moved with stealth and speed that almost wasn't human. His skin was considerably lighter than the man standing next to him, and maybe that was why I didn't notice how similar their features were until I was staring at the two men side by side.

I always knew they were kin of some kind but father and son? No, that was a surprise.

Mercy was 6'5" and a monster of a man. He intimidated others just by towering over most of them. He had me by only two inches, and I was kind of proud of that fact.

A black heart was tattooed under his right eye and attached to a web that pulled from the bottom corner and stretched the length of his neck to where a black widow spider crawled along most of his throat on the same side. Under the left eye were three teardrops for the three men he killed in prison to avenge the woman he loved and lost. It was a story most of us Ghosts knew about, but that didn't mean we had all the details. It wasn't hard to guess that woman was probably the mother of his children, now that I knew he had kids.

His barrel-shaped chest was covered in red flannel and a full-length black leather trench coat that brushed the top of the combat boots he always wore. Dark jeans wrapped his thick legs that resembled tree trunks more than limbs. MERCY was tattooed across the knuckles of his right hand, while another black widow spider covered the top of his left hand. All of his fingernails were painted black.

Peeking beneath the jacket were leather shoulder holsters that held at least two weapons. I was betting that the coat had multiple pockets that held more concealed within. Completely bald, he wore black sunglasses that were tugged off and shoved into a nearby pocket, exposing the icy blue color of his eyes. A rare attribute for a man of color. All of these characteristics made him seem larger than life.

His son favored him with a much lighter, honey-tinged complexion and didn't have the same tattoos. He held himself with similar confidence and that bold, ruthless nature. The eyes were different, though—a stormy gray. It should have clicked a lot sooner, and I felt like a fool for missing the details.

"Well, fucking hell. Now I see it."

Mercy chuckled with that deep rumble I knew well. The Jackal laughed, and it sent chills down my spine. I'd never want to meet either in a dark alley alone if I were a criminal. These men were lethal and didn't hesitate to take down those who preyed on the weak.

Mercy returned to his seat and gestured for his son to join us.

The Jackal sat on my right and stretched out, crossing his feet at the ankles. "Might as well introduce myself properly. I'm Darius Mayweather." He ticked his chin my way. "Pleasure to meet you, Staff Sergeant Grady Barnes."

"Damn. I wasn't expecting that," I admitted, shaking my head. "I think I need a drink."

Mercy let out a grunt in agreement and poured us each a shot of whiskey. Once we tossed the liquor back, the discussion turned serious.

"What do you need me to do?"

"Davina is in danger," Mercy revealed, filling his glass a second time and downing the shot before I could blink.

"My sister excels in finding trouble. We need to know she's got help if she decides to continue the path she's on."

"What kind of trouble?" I asked, wondering what the fuck this young woman was doing.

"Ever heard of the Black Market Railroad?"

Staring into Mercy's eyes, I nodded. "Shit. Yes."

"She's decided to fight them all on her own."

"Why would she do that?"

"Because she made a promise, and Davina never breaks her word. This won't be easy."

"Nothing ever is," I muttered, standing to my feet. "I'll find her."

"Good. I assumed you would."

"Because I'm dependable as fuck," I joked. "You got a recent picture of Davina?"

"Yeah," he grunted. "Texting it to you now."

My phone vibrated, and I swiped across the screen, staring down at the pretty young woman who looked like her brother's twin. Same honey complexion and stormy gray eyes. Curvy and fucking *gorgeous*. "I got it," I replied calmly, not betraying my reaction.

"Keep me informed, Ace."

"Will do," I agreed as I stood, heading outside to my Harley. Sliding on my shades, I smiled as I tucked the phone into the back pocket of my jeans.

Watch out, Davina. Ace is on the way.

PRESENT TIME—

TWITCHY WAS right. I came to the morgue because I'd been following her since the night I spoke to Mercy and the Jackal. Better known as the father and brother of Davina Mayweather. Dante Mayweather was a legend and a man I respected. He went by the name his fellow Marines gave him many years ago—Mercy. As in, he offered none. The man was ruthless.

His son took the alias the Jackal once he joined the other Ghosts. There were many more of us and a few of the Royal Bastards MC like Papa, who went by Avenger. I only knew that information because Mercy entrusted me with what I needed to know to help his daughter. Otherwise, I'd still be clueless.

As soon as I learned that Twitchy was going after the Russian human traffickers causing so much trouble in Nevada, I knew I had to accept Mercy's proposal. I expected to find a headstrong young woman with a chip on her shoulder and the grit of her father. I did.

What I didn't expect to find was a beautiful young woman who deeply cared for others and spent all of her free time helping victims. She was a Ghost without the title. The same passion and heart for those in need as her father and brother. She was sweet and spicy. Smart and lethal.

It only took me five days to find Davina Mayweather. Four to laugh at her wit. Three days to know she was special. Two to figure out she was tough as nails. One to lose my fucking heart.

I was one stupid motherfucker because I fell for this feisty, sexy, gorgeous, ballsy girl almost instantly, and there wasn't any way I was giving her up.

She wasn't just a job to me. Not another face like the women we saved on a daily basis. Abusive husbands. Rape victims. Domestic violence. Hope's Refuge was a safe haven.

But this goddess didn't need a thing from me other than my devotion, and I was already gladly giving it. She had no idea who the hell I was, and I should have been cautious, but my heart wasn't listening to my head. At least, not the one above my shoulders.

"I've been watching out for you for six months," I admitted, staring down and into the same pretty gray eyes as her brother. Long lashes fluttered as I held her tighter against me. My dick decided to join the party, and I couldn't help my reaction.

"Six months, and I've learned everything about you I need to know." My hand cradled the side of her face as I stared into those mesmerizing eyes. "You've got me as a backup in case shit goes south with the Russians, but that isn't why I'm kissing you. It's not the reason I can't stay away from you either."

She bit her lip, staring up at me with curiosity. "Well, don't leave me hangin'."

Never. "I've gotten to know you over the last six months. You know what I see?"

She frowned, placing her hands on my chest like she didn't want to hear my words. Too late.

"I see a strong, independent, brilliant woman with the purest, noblest heart I've ever had the pleasure of watching. I've met a lot of Ghosts through Hope's Refuge. None of those men, even with all of their good intentions and sacrifices, have the same level of commitment that you do. You don't back down, gorgeous. Not once. You stand for every single one of those victims. It's goddamn glorious."

She snorted. "You sure like to hear yourself talk."

A big stupid grin plastered across my mouth. "Yep. If it keeps you in my arms, you can bet on it."

Her smile wavered, and I caught the vulnerability she hid for the first time. "And the Russians?"

"I'm keeping tabs on that. So far, no reason to deviate in your plans."

"Then why did you show up now? What did Mercy say?"

There was a story there, and I wanted to dig for it but knew the timing was off. "He's concerned things are escalating. Mercy told me to move in."

"You mean he said it's time to bring me on board with all of this?" She sounded annoyed.

"I don't know what beef you have with Mercy, but it doesn't concern me. My job is staying by your side, and I intend to do that."

"I don't need a babysitter, Ace. I'm fully capable."

I didn't disagree. "I know you are," I replied with conviction, "but when those Russians come for you, it isn't going to be with a few men. They're going to send their best, and there's gonna be a fuck ton of them."

"Alright. We'll try it your way for now. I could use the time to catch up on my sleep. It's going to be hours before Bludge is up anyway. Keep watch, sexy bodyguard."

A chuckle escaped my lips as I watched her walking away, swishing that fine, rounded ass from side to side. I couldn't wait to give it a good smack and stick my tongue in her pussy. Bet she tasted just as spicy and delicious below as she did between her lips. It wasn't going to be long before I found out.

ROYAL BASTARDS MC

FOUR

Twitchy

"YOU SURE ABOUT THIS?" I asked Bludge, hanging my head as I learned the victim's identity. "She's a student at the same high school as Stefanie Holloway."

"Positive. Dental records are a match. She just had her wisdom teeth pulled six months ago."

"Son of a bitch!" I roared, picking up an empty stainless-steel bowl and chucking it across the room, not feeling any better when it hit the wall with a clang and then landed on the floor. "This can't be a coincidence. It must be the missing detail the police aren't releasing on the news. They're tracking this lead."

"Or they haven't figured it out yet," Ace pointed out.

"It's not like we can go in there and tell them how we know. We'll all be arrested," I complained, shaking my head. "This is awful."

25

"I'm handling this like the others," Bludge replied. "Anonymous drop-off. No one will know the connection, Twitch."

"That doesn't solve the problem, Bludge. Someone is providing girls to the Russians. I already tracked down the lead to the Scorpions. Shadow and the Royal Bastards are taking care of it. This is something different."

Both men nodded. Neither disagreed. The Scorpions weren't behind the kidnappings this time. This missing girl from the high school was a different case, even if the Russians were involved. I planned to find out exactly how this girl and Stefanie Holloway were connected. With that piece of the puzzle, I could determine what plan of action followed. There was no way I would let another young girl become a victim.

Since the night I saw that van around Halloween, I'd been tracking down the disappearances. Spotting Stefanie among them, I knew I had to help. But it was more than the shit going down with the Russians that spurred on my need for answers. I wanted to make the assholes pay who hurt my cousin Ronin. They were connected, the Scorpions MC members who slit his throat and killed his best friend and the Russians who were kidnapping young women. I needed to find out how that connection worked.

"I want to do a little recon."

Bludge shook his head, shutting the door on the fridge that held the female victim's body. She was ready for the family to confirm her identity, and this was the part I never stuck around to witness. "Risky, honey. You already know what I think. No point in rehashing how often we disagree."

"I still love you, Bludge."

He grunted, walking to the sink to remove his gloves and wash his hands. "That's cause I'm the sexiest motherfucker you know."

"Can't deny it," I answered with a wink. "You coming?" I asked Ace, raising a finger in the air and curling it a few times, so he followed me. "We have a school to scope out."

"Not the way I'd like," he deadpanned, and I couldn't help a giggle.

Ace sighed and then followed me out of the room as I blew a kiss to Bludge. He was used to my impromptu visits and flakiness, so he never cared how often I came and went or utilized his services. I paid him well. "Your funds will be available tomorrow," I announced as Bludge yelled out his thanks.

I quickly stopped to pick up my bag and then headed outside. The wind wasn't as brisk as last night, making it considerably less cold. I hopped into the SUV and flashed Ace a smile as he joined me.

"You look like you're brewing something up in that pretty head," he observed.

"I am. I need snacks. Lots of snacks. Boredom may just kill me without Twizzlers, chocolate, salty potato chips, and plenty of Cherry Coke."

Ace sat back against the seat, gesturing to the road. "Let's do it, babe. The night isn't getting any younger."

I loved the way he just gave in to my whims and desires as if it pleased him to make me happy. "Thanks, *babe*."

"I do like to hear endearments from those pretty lips. Of course, if you'd rather cry out my name, that's alright too."

"Oh, whatever." Men and their egos.

Half an hour later, we pulled up outside the school sans the lights and found a place to scope out the grounds without being seen. There weren't a lot of places to hide with all the desert cactus and tumbleweed, but we found a spot where other vehicles were parked and made sure to stay out of sight. An old building kept us mostly hidden from view.

For the first two hours, I went through half the snacks and a bottle of Cherry Coke. My supply needed to last, and I reluctantly closed all the packages, staring out at the star-filled Nevada skyline. Prettiest in all fifty states if you asked me.

I was bright and alert, anxious as I tapped my knee with my fingers.

"You doing okay, beautiful?"

"Never better, Ace."

After two hours, I was ready for anything. Unfortunately, boredom threatened to kill my jovial mood.

"Do you want to talk about anything?"

Staring over at Ace's mischievous grin, I figured he just had sex on the brain. "Like what?"

"Aren't you curious about me?"

Huh. Maybe he didn't just have sex on the brain. I definitely did. "How did you meet Mercy?"

"I thought you'd never ask." He cleared his throat, sitting up a little to stretch. "After I was discharged—"

"You're a Marine. I knew it. Haircut and demeanor gave you away. You guys are always ready to throw down."

He chuckled lightly, not the least bit put off that I interrupted him. "We sure are, beautiful. Anytime, anywhere, in and out of the sheets."

Rolling my eyes, I gave him a playful punch on the arm. "Okay. So you got out of the military and didn't have shit to do that was as meaningful as the Corps. Am I right? You needed to feel like you were making a difference."

"That's exactly right. How did you know?"

"It's how I would feel." I shrugged, pulling a licorice strip out of the bag and taking a huge bite. "I can't imagine enlisting young and leaving everything I know behind. How old were you when you signed up?"

"Eighteen. Fresh out of high school. I never regretted it. Gave eleven years to the Corps but felt I needed something more after that. I tried to make a living in the corporate world, but that isn't me. I like to get my hands dirty."

"And everything else," I mused, snickering.

"You bet your sexy ass." He winked and then ticked his chin my way. "What about you?"

"Life? Career? Goals?" I asked as he nodded. "Truth is, I don't know. I like my life the way it is. I have a lot of freedom, and I won't give that up. My independent nature is a gift from my father."

"That's the first time I've heard you refer to Mercy as your dad," he mused.

"That's because we have a rough relationship." Admitting that was opening a can of worms I didn't feel like discussing but only because it was old news. The past didn't define me. I preferred not to dwell on it.

"Define rough."

Sighing, I finished chewing my licorice and took a sip of my drink. "He likes to control me. I don't like to be controlled. That about sums it up."

"How old are you, sweetness? I'm thirty-six."

"Almost thirty-two," I answered with a smile. "Far too old to worry about this shit, but I do."

"Tell you what," he replied, reaching across the center console to grab my hand. He gave it a light squeeze and then intertwined our fingers. "You're an adult. You do what you want, Twitchy. Make your own heart happy, and the rest will fall in line."

"It's not that easy," I argued. "Not with Mercy or my brother."

"Then you keep livin', baby. One day to the next. They love you. Sooner or later, they're gonna realize that you're all grown up."

He had a point. "What if I just want to party, fuck, and get high all day?"

His lips twitched. "If you make sure I'm there, I won't let anything bad happen to you."

"You know I'm joking about the drugs." Not the rest, though.

He snickered, understanding precisely what I meant.

It had been a long time since I conceded any control at all in my life. Not to Darius or my father or even a boyfriend. I didn't like that weird buzz that hovered under my skin. The feeling that the walls were closing in, and I was about to be robbed of my free will. Always kept me at a distance from others.

Glancing at Ace, I didn't feel any of that, even with his hand clenching mine. I squeezed back and smiled at the tender look in his eyes. Maybe I finally found someone worth taking a risk for, someone who would love me without trying to dictate my decisions.

"You know what I want?"

He leaned closer, lifting his hand to caress the side of my face. "My lips on yours."

The kiss wasn't soft or sweet. Ace already understood me and how I worked. His mouth pressed to mine with a hunger I didn't expect but absolutely reciprocated. Our tongues collided as a soft moan left my throat. Nothing was sexier than a man who could anticipate what you liked and desired and fully deliver. I was willing to bet that he would rock my world between the sheets.

A sudden clatter outside the SUV startled us both.

"I think your hunch was right," Ace murmured as we separated. "We're not alone out here."

Both of us lowered in the seats, instantly on alert. When I pulled out my gun, Ace already had a 9mm in his hand. Neither of us was going to get caught by surprise.

"I don't regret that kiss, beautiful, but we should be careful."

Nodding, I agreed. "Does that mean you won't touch me the rest of the night?"

A mischievous grin flashed my way along with a dimple on his left cheek. "That just means we're not holding back when I get you alone. I want you, Twitchy. That isn't a secret. Unless I'm reading you wrong, I think you want me too."

"You're not wrong."

"Then focus on the present because later you aren't going to remember your name."

Shivering, I let out a shaky sigh. This man was positively wicked.

Clenching my thighs together, I lifted my chin and winked in his direction. "Good."

ROYAL BASTARDS MC

FIVE

Ace

"DON'T YOU DO IT," I whispered, watching Twitchy approach the docking bay where the school's daily deliveries were made. "Don't fucking go in there alone."

Did she listen? Hell no. That stubborn goddess held up a palm like that would stop me from joining her and shook her head.

"Motherfucker," I cursed.

I was going to spank her sexy little ass when this was all over, and it wouldn't be just for fun.

Five minutes ago, she spotted a black van pulling up to the school and backing up to the delivery dock. Two men dressed in dark suits exited and walked up the stairs, entering through the back door. The bay was still closed, and we didn't know what kind of business required their appearance, but it couldn't be good.

It was nearly one in the morning. No school received deliveries in the middle of the night.

Twitchy ordered me to stay put in the SUV as she slipped from the vehicle, and I cursed under my breath, gripping the steering wheel as I watched her moving through the shadows. It took everything I had not to go after her, but she needed to know I didn't think she was weak or incapable, and I had to fucking prove it.

Several more minutes had slowly faded before I opened the door and left anyway, worried she would end up in trouble or cornered. I'd hang back unless she needed me, but I couldn't allow anyone to harm her when I could prevent it. Maybe it was the Marine in me. Perhaps it was the control freak I'd become. None of that was the real reason.

Twitchy was my woman. It was that goddamn simple.

She could get pissed at me later for following her inside as I watched her sexy ass enter the same door as the two assholes in the dark suits. And she was absolutely gonna get frustrated when I dragged her ass out of that building if any shooting started. She might be tough, but she wasn't invincible. Bullet holes could kill her the same as me. Goddamn, I hated the thought of her in danger.

No wonder Mercy worried about his daughter. She was a firecracker through and through and chased down danger like she was a fucking member of the Avengers.

Keeping to the shadows as Twitchy had done, I made it to the building in less than two minutes, sneaking inside the same door. The heavy wood creaked slightly, and I hoped no one heard my clumsy entrance. I should have taken my time, but I was too concerned about that sexy little Harlot to slow down.

Raised voices in argument caught my attention as I stuck close to the walls, clearing each room I passed on the way to Twitchy. She didn't appear, and I hoped she wasn't already in trouble. My chest heaved as I sucked in a breath, hoping like hell she had the good sense to stay hidden.

At the next corner, I stayed put, noting it was a dead-end to my left, a wall to my back, and the same route I'd come from on my right. Straight ahead, the two men in suits were discussing something with a group of three additional men. The trio wore all black and spoke in a Russian accent. Fuck. No surprise there.

I hated being right, but the Russian bratva took root in Nevada decades ago, and now they operate in every major city in the state. I'd figured that out months ago while tracking Twitchy. That was why I didn't blink an eye when I saw all the suits. The shocking part was the female who joined them, strutting across the concrete floor in a tight dress to join the group.

My goddamn ex-girlfriend. *What the fuck?*

Sammy Cutter stood in a gold dress that did little to conceal her cleavage, hugging her body down to her knees, exposing her shapely legs and the expensive heels she wore. Blonde waves framed her face as she popped a hip and lifted her chin, flashing that fake smile men bought hook, line, and sinker. She was a flashy, greedy whore who sold herself to the highest bidder.

It shouldn't have been such a shock to see her sidle up to one of the Russians who grabbed her ass as he tugged her close, but it was. I thought she remained in Vegas when she ditched me for a high roller at one of the card tables in a casino during our weekend getaway almost a year ago.

Guess I was wrong.

The Russian smirked as he seized her chin, yanking it cruelly in his direction. "Sergei wants young, pretty girls. No sex workers or used up pussy."

"I understand," she purred, letting her hand dip down to his crotch.

He snatched her wrist with a snarl. "No games, little whore. Girls must be there on time."

"They will be," Sammy promised. "They have a volleyball game in Vegas. It's a small van with ten girls. Only two chaperones."

"All women?"

"Yes, Stepan."

The Russian's eyes lit up as I tensed, confident I was finding a way to stop these assholes from fulfilling their plan.

"Good. Sergei will be pleased."

One of the goons in the dark suit didn't look happy as he spoke. "What about our cut?"

Stepan turned in their direction, pulled a pistol from his jacket, and fired a shot into the guy's forehead. His companion reached for his weapon but wasn't fast enough. The bullet hit his heart, followed by three more as Stepan smiled with a cruel twist of his lips.

"This is why I hate Americans. No patience."

The two Russians next to him chuckled.

"Clean up this mess. Get rid of the bodies in the desert."

Sammy stood still, her hand trembling as she brushed the hair out of her face. I couldn't tell if she was shocked, scared, or worried about her own neck.

"Come, bitch. You will take my cock in every hole." Stepan started walking in my direction as I spun around, darting into one of the empty rooms in the hall. His phone rang, and he swiped across the screen, speaking in Russian as he turned the corner and stopped not ten feet from my position.

Shit.

I ducked behind an old desk, cursing silently as I wondered where Twitchy was hiding. She didn't make a noise or betray her location. I sent a text, but she didn't answer.

"Da," Stepan spat, pacing up and down the empty hall outside the room. More Russian phrases were spoken, but I only understood a few words.

Someone yelled loud enough for their voice to echo through Stepan's device. *"Nyet,"* he finally barked, cursing in English, "Fuck." He ended the call and grabbed Sammy's wrist, dragging her outside.

A soft sigh escaped as I glanced at my phone—no messages from Twitchy. I was about to lose my shit. The two Russians wrapped up the bodies and lugged them out of the school as I waited for the chance to leave. Twenty minutes later, the two goons cleaned up the blood, and no hint of the carnage remained. After the Russians left, I waited another ten minutes before I stood and stretched, cautiously sneaking around the building and whispering Twitchy's name. She never answered.

By now, I was pissed.

Deciding it didn't matter if I called her now or not, I dialed her number, but it went straight to voicemail. A few seconds elapsed before she finally replied.

Twitchy: I'm good.

Me: Where the hell are you?!

Twitchy: Inside the van.

Me: What van?

Twitchy: The black one, stupid.

For fuck's sake. Did she have a death wish?

Me: Do not tell me you're inside the fucking van that was parked outside the school.

Twitchy: Ok. I won't.

Motherfucker! What was the matter with my woman? Did she think she'd survive if they found her?

Me: Did they see you?

Twitchy: No. They dumped the bodies inside and drove off.

Pinching the bridge of my nose, I counted to twenty as I tried not to lose my temper.

Me: Where are you headed?

Speed walking to her SUV, I was relieved I still had the keys. Once inside, I started the ignition and pulled out of the lot, merging onto Hwy 95. When she didn't answer, I texted again.

Me: Where?

Twitchy: Desert. Outside of Tonopah. Halfway to Hawthorne.

Me: OMW

Slamming on the brakes, I pulled a quick U-turn and pushed down on the gas pedal hard. The vehicle lurched, gaining speed and momentum as I sped toward her destination.

Twitchy: Van turned left into the desert. Hurry!

Me: Got you, sweetheart. I'm right behind you.

Ten fucking minutes I wasted at that school. Long enough for the Russians to stop, open the back of the van, discover Twitchy hiding inside, and hurt her for getting into their business. My fist banged on the steering wheel twice as I muttered under my breath, cursing and trying not to panic.

I caught the dust the van kicked up to my left, thankful the wind prevented the sand from settling too quickly. It was fucking suicide to approach like this, but I didn't have time to lose. My headlights would reveal I was coming long before I reached them. The desert was black as tar tonight, even with the moon's silvery-gray light. Switching off the headlights wasn't an option.

Up ahead, I caught movement. The van's doors were open as I sped over cactus, tumbleweed, sand, and uneven ground. Bobbing up and down like a cork in water, I smacked my head on the roof of the damn SUV and gripped the steering wheel tighter, determined to reach Twitchy before it was too late.

Gunfire erupted as I skidded to a halt, pulling the SUV to the right.

The brakes nearly locked, and I swerved a few times before coming to a stop. I threw open the door and ran in her direction, watching as she crouched on one side of the van. She kept peeking around the doors, unloading bullets at a rapid pace. One of the Russians was hit in the chest, and he stumbled, falling to his knees before she fired a shot right between his eyes.

"Goddammit," I cursed, huffing as I pumped my arms and legs.

The other Russian was closing in on her location. He dodged around the front and then leaped in her direction, pulling the trigger on his weapon. Twitchy dropped as I cried out her name. For a heart-stopping second, I thought she was hit, but her hand lifted, and she fired off three shots as the Russian pointed his gun in my direction. Three bullets to the heart, and the Russian fell, dropping like a heavy sack of potatoes.

"Twitchy!"

She scrambled to her feet, dusting off her jeans as I approached. "What?"

"What the fuck was that?" I asked, gesturing to the van and the bodies.

"Justice?"

"This isn't funny. You didn't have to risk your life. You could have fucking died."

"I don't know what you're pissed about, Ace. Nothing happened. I'm fine."

She didn't look fine. Her hand was trembling as she holstered her gun. Adrenaline was pumping through her body, and she looked like she was about to fall over as she stumbled over her feet, leaning against the van's exterior as she sucked in a shaky breath.

"You're not fine."

ROYAL BASTARDS MC

SIX

Twitchy

"I DON'T KNOW WHAT you're pissed about, Ace. Nothing happened. I'm fine."

Denial sure was an easy alibi. The truth was, I didn't think this through and took an unnecessary risk. I just didn't want those assholes to get away with what they were doing.

Hitching a ride, I thought I could learn valuable intel. That was why I hopped into the back while those two idiots cleaned up their Russian boss's mess. They were careless and rushed, never noticing my presence. Recording the conversation taking place between the two Russian goons and someone over the phone, presumably Stepan, I hoped we'd learn of their plans once I had this bit of conversation translated.

"You're not fine," Ace growled, closing in as I leaned against the side of the van, shaking with the overload of adrenaline. It wasn't anything I hadn't experienced before.

"Back off, Ace." He was being irrational, and I didn't want to deal with his drama. That was why I always did shit on my own.

"You don't get to risk your life and make these kinds of choices without consulting me. We're a team. I get half the decision and opinion." He practically snarled his words as he slammed his hands onto the metal side panel, spanning either side of my head. "You. Could. Have. Died." He enunciated each word as his head lowered, his blue eyes darkening with emotion. The muscles in his upper arms bulged as he fought to maintain control.

"But I didn't," I pointed out, narrowing my eyes at his display of testosterone.

His fists thumped the metal exterior again as he growled, pushing up against me as his big body caged mine in. "Not the fucking point, Davina."

Blinking, I was caught off guard as my jaw dropped open and then snapped shut. He said my real name.

"You shouldn't have taken that risk! It's my job to keep you safe. How the fuck can I do that if you're going to do shit on your own?" His tirade didn't end there. "I work for Mercy. Dante Mayweather may have secrets, but I know most of them. I'm his top Ghost. His most trusted confidant, aside from Darius. He sent me to protect you. How the fuck am I supposed to do that if you hop in the back of a van and nearly get murdered?"

I didn't move, still stuck on the fact that he called me Davina and not Twitchy.

"You said my name," I whispered, staring up at him with wonder. "Why?"

Some of the anger dissipated with my softly voiced question.

"Because I wanted you to hear it. I need you to understand that I see the real you, Davina Mayweather. You're not just Twitchy or a Royal Harlot."

"You're not just the daughter of Dante Mayweather, the most respected man in the whole goddamn state. And you're not a piece of ass for a man to order around or just the pussy men want between your legs."

His little speech sparked something deep inside, and I swallowed hard. "Then what am I?"

"A sexy temptress. Beautiful goddess. Badass biker bitch. Intelligent woman. None of those matter the most."

"What does matter, Ace?" Searching his eyes, I suddenly wanted to know what I meant to him. Why did he chase me down and nearly lose his shit when I stepped into that van and risked my life?

"Grady," he grumbled.

"Huh?"

"Staff Sergeant Grady Barnes. My real name."

"Not just Ace?" I asked with a smirk.

"Not just Ace. Not to you, Davina."

Wow. I bit my lip, taking a good look at the hunky Marine in front of me. He was much more than I initially thought. Ace, Grady, was precisely the type of man I could build a future with, and that scared the shit out of me. Still, I couldn't help my curiosity. "Tell me what you meant a minute ago."

One of his hands lowered and drifted across my shoulder, caressing the skin across my neck before he leaned in, his mouth hovering a few inches from my lips.

"You've burrowed down inside me, sweetness. Taken root and attached to my bones and muscles. I'm not sure how you managed it, but you've carved a place in my heart that no other woman has been able to reach. It's not easy for me to admit that."

I opened my mouth to ask why when he shook his head, pressing a finger to my lips.

"I'm a tough man. It's been bred in me since I joined the Corps. I don't do mushy feelings or sweet pillow talk. I like things rough and fast, especially with women. That changed the first time I saw your flirty smile and sassy attitude. I was fucking gone after that."

"You sure are admitting a lot for a guy who doesn't know what I think or feel. Cocky bastard," I joked, leaning into his palm as he cupped my cheek.

"Never been a guy who preferred slow and gentle. Just not my style. But I could learn to appreciate it with you, my goddess."

"Grady?"

He closed his eyes briefly and then reopened them, focusing on my lips. "Yeah, baby?"

"I don't do mushy or slow and gentle either."

The corners of his lips twitched. "Knew that, precious, but if you change your mind, let me know."

Tilting my head to the side, I reached out and grabbed his stiff dick, appreciating the size. He wasn't lacking in that area. "Fuck me, Grady. Fuck me right here in the middle of the desert up against this van, and don't stop until I come all over your cock."

His mouth crashed down on mine so hard my teeth nearly rattled. My back slammed into the cool metal surface as he stripped off my leather jacket, tossing it aside. Fabric ripped as he tugged off my shirt and then unclasped my bra, all in the time it took for me to gasp a couple of ragged breaths. This man knew exactly what he was doing, and I couldn't wait to reap the rewards.

His tongue slid across my left breast as he lowered his head, sucking on the nipple before he bit at the flesh, drawing the bud into his mouth. My body jolted as my fingers slid across his scalp, skimming the roughness on the shaved sides of his head and kneading the back of his neck as my back arched.

"Fucking perfect tits," he murmured as he switched to my other breast, sucking hard on the skin of my cleavage, marking the span of both breasts as I moaned. "Gonna leave my mark all over you and my cum between your thighs. Fucking leave no doubt that you're mine."

"Yes," I agreed on a sigh, loving the way his hands grabbed and clutched at my body, touching me everywhere he wanted.

"Need inside you. Right fucking now."

"Then do it. I want your cock, Grady. Give it to me."

Unbuttoning my pants, I shoved down the zipper as he followed my lead. My boots and jeans were tossed aside as his pants dropped to his knees, and my sexy Ace picked me up. On instinct, I wrapped my legs around his waist, digging my heels into his ass.

"Goddamn gorgeous, baby. That's what you are from head to toe. I'm gonna feast on your pussy later, so don't go thinkin' I forgot about it."

He held me close, my breasts crushed to his chest, my body pinned against the van as his hand slid down my underwear and beneath the top edge. Three fingers dove into the warmth and through my slit, swiping up the dampness of my arousal.

"So fucking wet for me." He tasted the wetness on his fingers and growled. "So good."

"Fuck me, Ace. I want you to make me scream."

The material ripped as he shoved the silk aside and lined up his dick. There weren't any sweet words spoken, and I didn't need them. He'd already said enough. What I needed—*what we both needed*—was to feel one another.

I cried out when his thick shaft plunged inside me with a single brutal thrust, burying deep as he held my hips and then slid out, ramming back home again. The pace was brutal. Beautiful. Relentless.

Nikki Landis

He didn't stop, and I didn't want him to slow down. He pumped into me as I bounced up and down on his dick, and I forgot everything—almost my fucking name.

Holding onto his shoulders, my fingernails dug into the thick muscle as my core clenched. He was hitting that perfect spot, and I grew wetter in response, dripping onto his dick as he grunted his approval. I knew my orgasm wasn't going to take long. I could feel the pressure intensifying as the sweat began to build on my skin. Cold air brushed across my nipples as they hardened, and I tossed my head back, swiveling my hips in desperation.

"Give it to me, baby. Fucking come all over my dick."

He didn't touch my clit. Didn't need to, and that was a first. Usually, I had to beat my own nubbin hard to get off like this. Not with Ace.

A primal, emotional eruption burst from within as I cried out, clenching hard around his cock before I screamed his name with my release. It came on fast and fierce, wracking my body in a cluster of shudders as my legs shook, and I couldn't stop shouting his name. My hips pistoned in a perfect pace with Ace's, and we rocked against one another, groaning with both passion and pleasure. His hands gripped my hips hard enough to leave bruises, but I didn't mind. Watching this man lose his control was a marvel to behold.

I'd heard it said in the past that only women come with an expression drenched in ecstasy and fulfillment, that men look distorted and pained if not downright strange. Not my Ace. Sheer satisfaction stretched across his handsome features, followed by a look of pure devotion. His final thrusts joined us in a way I would never forget as he came hard, pressing his mouth to mine in a thoroughly intoxicating kiss. The kind of kiss you get before sex and not after, but that didn't matter to Ace.

He lifted his head as our lips parted and then pressed another kiss on the tip of my nose. "You're done now, goddess. I'm addicted to this pussy, and I'm fucking you every chance I get."

Laughter tumbled from my lips, and I sighed happily, leaning in to hug him tighter. "I'll hold you to it."

ROYAL BASTARDS MC

SEVEN

Ace

"**W**E NEED TO TALK about what happens next," I murmured, dropping a kiss on top of Davina's head.

"The sex or the bodies?" Humor twinkled in her eyes as she gave me a wicked smile. "Because I'm good with the sex. Lots of it. You've got a standard to maintain now."

I couldn't help the dark chuckle that escaped as I shook my head, leaning back as I watched her reaction. "No, precious. This is different."

Thirty minutes ago, we left the desert after tossing the Russian corpses into the van and torching it. The night sky lit up with flames as dark smoke billowed into the air, signaling the fire for miles. Scavengers and predators wouldn't be the only ones to investigate.

We were counting on the fact that Stepan would learn about this, and the Russians would be pissed.

Maybe that was tipping them off, but I didn't give a shit. I preferred to fight my enemy the way I did overseas. No mercy.

"I'm not letting you go off and get yourself killed, so we need a plan."

She sighed, briefly dropping her head back against the headrest before nodding. "Okay."

Surprised she gave in that easily, I gave her a stern look. "I mean it."

"I know you do, Ace. You're right. If we're going to save these girls, we can't be careless or unprepared. We're going to need a little help, starting with the conversation in Russian that I recorded."

Impressed, I leaned in and stole a kiss. "Damn, baby. You're fucking resourceful."

"You have no idea," she teased. "I'm calling my pres."

"Go for it."

Sliding across the screen on her cell, she opened her contacts and clicked on Inferno's name. The line rang twice before she answered.

"Twitchy," Inferno moaned, grunting as I heard something wet in the background.

"What the hell, pres," Twitchy gushed, glancing at me with a shrug. "Catch you at a bad time?"

"Just getting fucked in the ass."

Damn. These girls didn't pull any punches.

"Is that figuratively or metaphorically?" Twitchy's lips curved into a grin. "Because either way sounds painful."

"Girl, I got a busted pipe in the bathroom of the clubhouse, and the goddamn plumber has ass crack gapping from here to Nevada. I can't unsee that shit."

A laugh tumbled from my lips as I shook my head.

"Pres, you made my day," Twitchy announced, her eyes twinkling with amusement.

"Shit. I really don't want to see this guy's brown eye. Know what I'm sayin'?"

"I do."

Sharp laughter erupted from my woman's chest, and I smiled at the affection I could hear in her voice. She cared for Inferno and the rest of the Harlots.

"What you need, Twitch? Something is up. I can feel it."

Twitchy sighed. "Lots of shit to deal with. Calling you before I talk to Duchess."

Inferno's voice softened. "What kind of trouble are you in? How can I help?"

"Know that trafficking ring causing problems here in Nevada?"

"The Black Market Railroad, right? Thought the Royal Bastards had that cleared up."

"They're working on it, pres, but I stumbled upon another dead girl. She was buried in Stefanie Holloway's grave. I helped shadow find his girl Stefanie in Vegas after she was taken, remember?"

"Yeah, I remember."

"Bludge identified the remains."

Inferno snorted over the phone. "How's my favorite slice and dice man?"

"Cranky and lovable as ever. You know how Bludge is. The girl in the grave went to the local high school. The same school that Stefanie attended. No way that's a coincidence."

"Shit," Inferno cursed. "What now?"

"I staked out the high school last night. Guess who was there?"

"Fucking Russians," Inferno spat. "Anyone else?"

"Yeah. A couple of goons in dark suits. I still don't know every piece of the puzzle. It'll have to wait."

"What are you not telling me, Twitchy?"

I placed a hand on my woman's shoulder and squeezed, giving silent support. "Go ahead," I whispered.

"Found out one of the Russian leaders is Stepan. Sergei Resnikov obviously brought in more men to replace the ones the Royal Bastards took out. It's a goddamn mess."

"Motherfucker!" Inferno sounded pissed.

"Stepan shot the two suits that showed up last night to meet him. They tossed the bodies in a van and drove them into the desert. Not sure what affiliation they had. Looked like the law of some kind even with the cheap suits they wore."

"What did you do, Twitchy? My Spidey senses are all tingly."

Spidey senses? What was up with that? A Spiderman joke between the two women?

"I hopped in the back and hitched a ride. Shot both of them when we stopped, then torched the van with all the bodies."

"I don't know whether to be pissed, impressed or throttle your dumbass for risking your life like that."

Giving my woman an I-told-you-so look, I crossed my arms over my chest.

Twitchy flipped me off and made a face.

"It was worth it. I recorded a conversation they had in Russian. I'm betting it's got crucial details we need to prevent another kidnapping."

"Fuck. What kidnapping?"

"Stepan mentioned a van full of high school girls. Young, pretty, and innocent. He'll sell them to the highest bidder, pres. I can't let that happen."

Inferno sighed. "No. None of us can. Let me grab Georgia."

"That's part of the reason I called."

The phone was muted, and I turned to Davina, caressing the line of her jaw. "We're going to help those girls. Don't worry."

"I know that, Ace. I hate not knowing how many others are at risk. Sure, we save these girls, but how many more will be taken, and we'll never know until it's too late?"

Her voice cracked, and I tilted her chin up, pressing a soft kiss on her lips. "Remember, this isn't just one battle. It's a fucking war."

"You'll go to war with me, Ace?"

"You bet your sexy ass I will, baby."

"YOU'RE TOO GOOD TO be true," I teased, nibbling on Ace's lips. "Thank you."

"Like I'd miss the opportunity to fuck up those Russian assholes."

I was about to reply when a husky twang greeted me and took the phone off hold. "Hello, sexy mama. What you got for me?"

"If it isn't my Georgia peach. How are you, sugar?" I asked, flirting with one of my favorite sisters in the club.

"A whole lot better if'n you bring that sexy ass of yours back to the clubhouse."

I couldn't help the small laugh that followed. "Don't go talkin' sweet and get me all hot and bothered."

"Got plenty of toys to help you get off, honey," she drawled in that sensual tone she was known for. It made me wish I was bisexual just to sample all that fun she always promised.

"Wish this was a pleasure call, Georgia. I've got a Russian conversation I need translating. You up for it?"

"Of course, skinny britches. I've got a pad and a pen. Play the recording whenever you're ready."

Bringing up the video I'd taken while hiding in the back behind the bodies, I hit play.

Georgia remained silent for a minute and then asked me to pause. "Hold on. Can you back that up? I want to double-check what the boss one just said."

"How far do you need it backed up?"

"About twenty seconds."

I backed up the recording, noticing the only visual was the back seats in the stolen van. I'd held my cell and turned it toward the front to ensure the audio was clear. Luckily, those stupid thugs never turned on the radio. They were far too busy on the phone for most of the trip. My battery almost died, but I had ten minutes of Russian dialogue for Georgia to analyze.

When the recording ended, Georgia heaved a big sigh. "First half wasn't all that important. Discussion about the shooting, the bodies, burying them out in the desert for scavengers to find. Shit like that. Figured you already knew that stuff since you spoke to Inferno about the bodies. The men kept referring to an incoming shipment with girls. Someone named Sergei was in the background. He talked about high-value product and moving them out of the U.S."

"That's what I was afraid of."

Ace squeezed my hand, and I knew he was worried about it too.

"The one on the phone kept talking about Stepan and some plan everyone disagreed on. They argued over the transportation of new girls. Sergei wanted to keep his contacts in Canada, filtering the merchandise through the border. According to the two men in the van, Stepan argued it was too risky. When they informed Sergei, he got pissed. Stepan and Sergei don't like one another, for what it's worth. Someone higher up in the organization required them to work together. A man named Gorbachev. Whoever he is, they all respected him."

"Never heard of him," I admitted, "but maybe Grim has. It's worth talking to the Royal Bastards about it."

"They're picking up the girls tomorrow during their trip to Vegas. Stepan plans on following their vehicle until they're halfway to sin city with nothing but desert around for miles. They'll hit the vehicle from behind. When the women stop, they'll shoot the chaperones and take the girls. They'll be pushed into a truck in less than a few minutes and driven north."

"Never to be heard from again," I replied, turning to Ace.

He shook his head. "We'll stop them," he mouthed without a noise.

"I heard them say the route goes through Carson City."

"Thanks, Georgia. Could you put Inferno back on?"

"You got it, honey lips. Be seein' ya real soon."

There was a pause, and then I heard my pres. "We're packing up and heading your way, Twitch. Meet you at the Crossroads. Give me about six hours."

"Wil do, pres. Ride safe."

The call ended, and I sighed, annoyed, when I noticed a slight headache pulsing between my eyes.

"We need to find someplace comfortable for a few hours. A shower, a hot meal, some vigorous sex, and then you call the Duchess. Grim can wait too. You're gonna fall over in a minute if you don't get a nap in."

"I'll be alright, Ace. Duchess can't wait. It's too important, but I'll take you up on the shower and everything else."

"Thought you would. Let's find a hotel."

Ace booked us a room, and we parked in the back, backing the SUV into the space in case anything went down and we needed to leave in a hurry. We didn't have much baggage, only a duffel bag, a backpack, and a small suitcase. My oversized Michael Kors handbag added to the meager amount of luggage. Neither of us was overly concerned about our wardrobe. We managed, and if something needed replacing, then we bought it.

I stifled a yawn as Ace closed the door and locked it, flopping onto the king-sized bed we were sharing. After our romp in the desert, it hardly mattered if we shared a bed. A girl really couldn't complain after being fucked like that. I sure wanted to experience it again.

"You certain you don't want to close your eyes for a few minutes, sweetness?"

Lifting my head, I caught the concern he didn't bother to hide. "Not yet. I need to call Duchess."

"Make it quick, or I'll sweep you beneath the covers, and then you won't have a choice."

Patting his cheek, I winked at his playful tone. "Honey, it's sweet you think you're in control."

Ace blew out a breath. "You ride my cock later, and I'll forgive you for that."

"Done."

ROYAL BASTARDS MC

EIGHT

Twitchy

"DAMN GIRL, WHERE YOU been?"

It had been far too long since I heard my best friend's voice. Life had gotten in the way, and I missed how we used to have all the time in the world to talk about guys, our future, and ruling the road as Harlots. I missed having her close enough that I could walk to her house, and by the tone of her voice, I could tell she felt the same. Stephanie Winters was as close to me as a sister. I rarely called her anything but her road name now, but she'd always be Stephanie to me.

"Hey, Duchess. Gettin' around. You know me."

"Sure do, babe. You doin' alright?"

"Wish I could say yes."

"Fill me in." Duchess had this no-nonsense way about her that made you want to spill your guts. She was quiet, precise as a rattlesnake before it struck a target, and twice as lethal.

"You know all the shit with the Russians and trafficking and the bullshit in Nevada?"

"That's still a fucking issue? What about Grim and the Bastards?"

I had to laugh because Inferno said the same thing. Grim would be pissed if he knew the Harlots were questioning his ability to handle business. Not that we didn't think he was capable. Quite the opposite. Those Reapers dealt with shit on a whole different level than most of us, and that was no joke.

"He's working on it. I'm meeting with him in a few hours."

"Okay. That's not the problem, is it?"

"No. Inferno is coming from Cali tomorrow. Russians are planning to kidnap a van full of girls."

"What the hell? How did you learn about that?"

I went through everything that happened in the last twenty-four hours, waiting for her response once I finished.

"Well, that's fucked up."

"No shit, babe."

"The balls on these Russians. No way we're letting them take those girls."

"Didn't think you would," I replied, relieved that she was on her way, joining without waiting for an invitation. Not that she needed one. Duchess went wherever she pleased.

We would need all the help we could get now that we decided to get involved. Not like I hadn't already done that when I hopped in the back of that van. Shooting two of those assholes cemented my involvement. I didn't regret it either.

"Keep an eye out. Roulette and Paramore will want in on the fun too."

"Got a bottle of Fireball with your name on it." We used to down shots of Fireball and chased them with Patrón when the Harlots first became a club. Those were some wild days.

"Oh, I'm counting on it."

Duchess ended the call, and I flopped back on the bed, releasing a sigh as my eyes fluttered. Warm hands reached out and tucked my body close, wrapping me up as I cuddled into Ace's chest.

"Just two hours. That's all we've got," I murmured as he pressed a kiss to my forehead.

"I already set the alarm. Hitting the timer now." His grip tightened as I released a contented sigh. "Sleep, precious. I've got you."

A SHRILL, BLARING WAIL woke me from the depths of slumber, and I shoved the source, snickering when I realized I nearly pushed Ace off the bed. He grumbled a sexy growl and pounced, pestering kisses all over my face as I squealed at him to stop.

"Revenge, my sweet. I almost landed my naked ass on the carpet."

Naked? Opening my eyes, I stared down at the jeans he was still wearing. "Such a cock tease."

"I remember hearing that you were addicted to my dick."

"Your dick? I said cock. There were no specifics."

Ace rolled me over and smacked my ass. "There's only one cock in your life now. Mine. Get used to it."

Pouting, I pretended to be upset. "But I love all kinds of dicks."

His eyes narrowed. "Baby, I'll gladly pick up all the toys you desire. Tell me what you want, and I'll buy it. We can experiment and have fun, but the only real cock filling your pussy is gonna be mine."

"Is that so?" I asked, trying hard not to smile.

"Damn fucking sure."

"Such a caveman."

"You love it." His expression grew solemn as both of his hands cradled my face. "You're all I want, Davina. If this is just a fling for you, I'm okay with that. I'll take whatever I can get. I might get my big ass all heartbroken, but I don't want any other woman than you."

"Shut up." Slipping my hand around his neck, I pulled his face closer to mine. "You're all I want too. Kiss me, you idiot."

Ace's lips met mine in a tender, passionate kiss that nearly made my toes curl. Sometimes, this man surprised me in all the right ways.

"Can we fuck?" I asked, batting my eyelashes at him.

"Christ. Get naked. We need to shower before it gets too late."

"Not even a quickie?"

"Don't make me spank your ass again."

Silly giggles left my lips as I slid from the bed and stripped, watching Ace's eyes darken with hunger.

"Fuck."

"What?" I asked innocently.

"Nothing but blue balls, apparently."

"I didn't say no to sex. You did."

"We don't have the time," he mumbled, staring at the juncture between my thighs. "Fuck it. Get in the damn shower. I can't go all day without coming. It'll fuck me up."

I couldn't hold back as more laughter erupted from deep in my belly. No man ever made me feel as light and happy as Ace did. I was one dark girl most of the time. Because of Ace, that was becoming a part of the past. It was more than just the humor and the fact that he kept me on my toes. There was something honest and heartfelt about the way he touched me and used all those endearments. A sincerity that mixed with affection and respect. He didn't want to change me and accepted my independence with a grace most men couldn't grasp.

Ace was the most complex and intoxicating man I'd ever met.

He started the shower and let the water grow warm, adjusting the temperature before he reached for my hand and tugged me inside. Under the steady spray, he dampened the dark curls on my head and gently lathered them, rinsing out the shampoo before applying conditioner.

"You're good at this," I observed, wondering how many women he practiced on in the past.

"I learned a long time ago. My sister's little girl had a head full of thick curls like this when she was little."

"That's adorable, Ace."

He flashed a tight smile, and I wondered what was wrong.

"She died when she was eight. Leukemia." He swallowed hard as I slid my arms around his neck. "Never told anyone. I haven't spoken of Laura and Amy since before I enlisted. I'm not sure why I'm telling you now."

"Sometimes, you just have to let the things that bottle up inside you loose. When it's time, you let go, and the hurt doesn't ache as much anymore."

Ace's mouth covered mine as he kissed me, thrusting his tongue inside as he deepened the kiss. My back met the tiled wall as he forced a knee between my thighs, opening them wider. One hand slapped against the tile next to my head while the other cupped my breast, kneading the soft tissue as the kiss continued.

I moaned as he tweaked my nipple and slowly let his fingers dive down my belly and over my mound. Sliding two fingers through the slit, he hissed as he circled my clit, then sank lower to breach the walls of my pussy.

My back arched as he plunged in and out, stroking that sensitive area with expertise. His palm kept brushing the nubbin above, and I bit my lip as my hips began to rock back and forth. In and out, he glided those fingers through my cream and locked eyes, never looking away. He enjoyed watching my reactions as I lifted my hands and squeezed my breasts, groaning with the building pleasure within.

Ace grunted as I noticed the hard length of his dick bobbing between us.

"You fucking me or not?"

Emboldened by my words, his fingers slid from my sheath, and he licked them clean, spinning me around and placing my hands on the wall. Warm water fell over my head and shoulders as he tilted my hips. Ace filled me in one swift stroke, thrusting inside me as I bent over more to accommodate his hard, eager dick. His cock pistoned in and out, taking me savagely from behind as I cried out repeatedly and tried to match every thrust with my hips.

I was close to coming when he pulled out, and I turned around, loving the wicked gleam in the depths of his blue eyes.

"I love fucking you," he announced, picking me up as my legs wrapped around his waist. He pinned me up against the tile and thrust back inside, ramming his stiff rod at an almost brutal pace until something changed. His tempo eased, and he moved slower, gliding in and out as if he no longer wanted to hurry. His lips met mine, and we hardly noticed the temperature of the water growing cooler.

"I love you, Davina. Yeah, it's probably too soon to say it, but I don't give a fuck. Holding back isn't in my nature."

"It's not in mine either," I admitted.

"I'm aware, my perfect goddess."

"I think I love you too."

"Don't say it unless you mean it. I'm far too easy to please."

His joke meant to keep things light, but I wasn't lying. "I do, Grady. I'm falling hard for you."

"Then keep falling," he quipped with a cheesy grin.

Both of us smiled, and then he picked up the pace again, pressing down on my clit as I dug my nails into his skin, coming so hard a minute later that I wailed his name. A deep growl rumbled in his chest as he pumped his hips a few more times and then filled me up, jets of his cum spurting inside me as I clung to his upper body, lifting my chin for the kiss I knew he wanted.

Both of us were panting as he held me against him, turning the faucet until the water wasn't cold anymore. "Need to ask something that's been on my mind."

"Okay."

"What was Inferno talking about with the whole Spidey senses thing?"

"You wait until I'm naked and your thick cock is poking between my thighs before you ask that?"

A smirk crossed his handsome features. "Maybe I was just getting you relaxed first."

"You didn't fuck me stupid," I pointed out, mildly amused. "Would you believe me if I told you something that seemed impossible?"

"I would believe anything you told me. The sky is actually purple? Done. Candy is really salty, not sweet? Okay. You have Spiderman's abilities? Nope. I draw the line there. You can't fuck with Marvel."

"Are you sure you're not an alien? I've never met a guy like you."

"I find it offensive that you don't take Marvel characters seriously."

I slapped him on the arm. "Ace."

His eyes twinkled as he leaned in and kissed me. "Okay. I'm listening."

"My family is special. My father and brother can do the same thing that I can. You've probably noticed that Mercy often seems to know things far in advance. He can predict what will happen, and he's rarely wrong. Darius is just as gifted."

Ace blinked, taking it all in.

"My family has the gift of sight. It works differently for each of us. I don't get visions, but I know when something is going to happen—good or bad. I can sense when I need to make decisions and what those are, and I can tell how much my choice will affect the outcome. That's why I took the trip in the van and snuck in the back. I knew I wouldn't die."

"Wow," he whispered. "That's amazing."

A timid smile appeared on my lips.

"And reckless not to tell me. I worried for nothing, precious. Probably gave me a few more gray hairs."

"Whatever."

Ace pressed both hands against my face, staring intensely into my eyes. "I don't care if you turn green, glow, have a monster living inside you like Venom or spin tiny webs. You're my Davina. That's it. Your secrets are safe with me."

Fuck. This man really was working his way deep into my heart.

"Good. I don't want to tell my father you know the family secret. He might kill you."

Ace smirked. "Not this sexy motherfucker. I'll just marry his daughter and join the family."

My mouth popped open in shock. "You're serious?"

"As a heart attack, baby. Sooner or later, you'll be tattooed on my body and wear my ring on your finger. If you don't believe me, those Spidey senses should confirm it."

I waited for any feeling to contradict his words. None came.

ROYAL BASTARDS MC

NINE

Ace

Twitchy practically bounced up and down in her seat as we pulled up to the front gate of the Crossroads. She pointed to the lot and moaned with pleasure when she saw her Harley parked at the end of a low row, the chrome and shiny metal glittering in the late morning sunshine. True to the Nevada desert, it was already warm even in late December. The temperature fluctuated quite a bit this year, and we seemed to be having an unusual heatwave.

The window rolled down, and a kid who couldn't be more than twenty gave us the stink eye. "Guess I know what happened to the missing SUV now. Grim's gonna be pissed, Twitchy."

"Yeah, yeah. He'll get over it. How you been, Spook?"

He shrugged, glancing toward the clubhouse. "Worried about Toad, if I'm honest. You talk to him lately?"

"No." All teasing disappeared from her face. "What's up with my cousin?"

"You should ask Grim."

"I'm asking you."

Spook shook his head. "Don't need any shit from my pres. Talk to Grim."

Twitchy slumped against the seat as the gate opened, and we pulled onto the lot. I parked in one of the spaces in front of the auto repair shop. Reaper's Custom Rides & Repair was well known throughout the state.

Personally, I thought it was clever that they used that logo along with the grim reaper riding a Harley. Catchy if you ask me. They had a reputation for working on motorcycles and hot rods but also performed regular automobile maintenance. Kept their noses clean, according to gossip.

As I exited the vehicle and met with these bikers for the first time, I began to wonder if the other rumors I heard were true—a rough-looking bunch in leather and lots of tattoos, beards, and chains. One guy resembled the devil with red and black face paint and dressed all in dark denim. Someone referred to him as Diablo, and I didn't doubt he had the personality to match it.

Twitchy sauntered ahead of me through the front doors, waving at a few club members along the way. She was bold and didn't hesitate to strut to the bar, demanding a drink. Amused, I knew she was a Harlot, and since they were affiliated with the Royal Bastards, that meant this was her clubhouse in a way. A home away from home.

The Crossroads was infamous for debauchery, wild parties, and numerous other tawdry affairs, but as I surveyed the common room, bar, pool tables, and the rest of the décor, I doubted most of those rumors were true. People liked drama and embellished their stories for nothing more than a few laughs.

"Grim," Twitchy hollered, slapping a big guy with blond hair that brushed the top of his shoulders on the back, swallowing a shot of whiskey. "How you been, you cranky fucker?"

He snorted, gesturing to the room. "Livin' the life, Twitch. Finally bring back my SUV?"

"Yep." She snatched the shot of hard liquor pushed in her direction and slammed it down, asking for another. Two shots in, she appeared to lose a little of the tension in her shoulders.

Grim watched her closely as if dissecting a complicated puzzle. "What's wrong, Twitchy?"

She turned his way, glancing around the room. A tall guy with a dark beard flashed her a smile, his arm around a buxom brunette. They headed over to my woman as she smiled.

"Wraith! Tawni! So happy to see you both."

She hugged Tawni and leaned back, opening her mouth to speak, when a young man with a limp appeared, sporting dark shaggy hair and a seriously dark aura.

"Twitchy! Stefanie was just asking about you."

"Shadow! Damn, everyone is here today, huh? Where's your pretty girl at?"

"Asleep." He swallowed hard, ticking his chin toward Grim. "A discussion for another day. Talk to pres. He'll help."

My eyes widened as I realized he knew why she was here. To my knowledge, she never contacted him, so this was more than a little bizarre.

"I will, Shadow. Promise."

"Don't delay. It has to be now."

She nodded, giving him a hug before turning back to Grim. "We got some shit to discuss. It's important." Turning my way, she waved me over. "This is my guy, Ace. You can trust me."

Grim reached out a hand, and I shook it. "Ace."

"Grim. Glad to finally meet."

He arched a brow, wondering what I meant. "I'm a Ghost for Mercy."

"Ah, yes. I should have realized that when you walked in. You got that same aura as Papa. No bullshit. Military. Protective to a fault."

I chuckled at his accurate description. "That about sums it up."

"Need a drink? Sounds like we got a lot to discuss."

Shaking my head, I knew I needed to keep a clear head. "Maybe later."

He stood, placing a hand on my shoulder. "I'll hold you to it." Two fingers lifted to his mouth as he blew a sharp whistle. "Everyone out but Rael and Mammoth."

The common room emptied except for two men I didn't notice before now. The first was the biggest motherfucker I'd ever seen in my life. He had to be six and a half feet tall with shoulders so vast they were practically the size of a small car. A long beard reached his chest as he narrowed his eyes in my direction.

Grim gestured to the mammoth of a man. "My VP, Mammoth."

The name fit.

Another biker strolled forward, grinning with a smile that was far too sadistic. Maybe it was the fact that he was the only other club member I'd seen wearing face paint, or perhaps it was the fact that he looked like a demented skeleton.

Black and white makeup made him appear as a ghostly reaper. I wasn't sure what look he was going for, but it certainly made him seem intimidating. Not that I gave a shit. His gothic appearance didn't spook me.

He didn't say a word but charged forward and stopped a couple of inches from my face, standing toe to toe as if he expected me to flinch or back down. I didn't move a muscle or blink. Just held my stance while my lips slowly curled in amusement.

He reminded me of a few guys I served with during active duty. They were all show and got a kick out of their position. This guy was cocky as fuck, but I didn't dislike him.

"Damn. I like Ace already, Twitch. He's a pretty fucker too," the biker finally blurted.

A snicker left my lips as he took a few steps backward, leaning against a nearby pool table.

"My SAA, Rael." Grim shot Rael a smirk. "He loves to entertain himself."

Twitchy shook her head. "Don't encourage him. Rael thrives on that shit."

I didn't doubt it.

Grim sat at one of the nearby tables with a bottle of whiskey. He poured five shots and passed them around as we took our seats. My woman sat on my lap, placing her glass on the table once it was empty. Grim poured another, settling back in his seat as Twitchy sighed.

"The Black Market Railroad is still in Tonopah, and I know the name of the Russian in charge. The guy over Sergei Resnikov."

Grim leaned forward, his jaw clenching hard. "Tell me."

"Gorbachev."

Mammoth growled as he got up and began to pace, heaving his bulk around with every step.

Rael's lip curled into a snarl. "Tell us what you know."

Twitchy explained her story a third time, leaning over the table when she finished.

"We've got to stop this Russian prick Stepan. He's as dangerous as Sergei. These traffickers don't care how many they hurt. They've got connections all over the state, and they don't fear anyone."

"How long do we have before they go after the girls?" Grim seemed tense, and I couldn't blame him. I was wound tight for the same reasons.

"About four hours. Thanks to the conversation Georgia translated, I've got the route they'll take."

"Four hours? Fuck, Twitch. Nothin' like waitin' until the last goddamn minute, huh?"

She flipped off Rael for his comment and didn't bother to answer.

"Pres," Mammoth called out, "Gotta know what you want. Right fucking now. Can't delay on this."

Grim tossed back the whiskey he'd been holding onto and slammed the glass down on the wooden surface. "We keep our club and ol' ladies safe. This is a fuckin' war, brothers. Has been for a long while now. So if we got to fight another battle, we do it."

Rael's fist pumped in the air as Mammoth gave a sharp nod.

"We won't be alone. Harlots are coming too," Twitchy announced.

Grim blew out a breath. "Which Harlots?"

"Duchess insisted on being here. Inferno too."

"Which means Roulette, Paramore, Georgia, and Indigo," Rael added.

"Of course."

I heard of all the Harlots but Indigo and figured she was from the same Cali chapter as Twitchy.

"What's your part in this?" Rael asked, sitting down across from me. "Fucking Twitch doesn't mean you're loyal to the rest of us."

He had a point, even if I didn't like it. Leveling him with a hard stare, I told him the truth. "Since I love this feisty little Harlot, that's my first priority. No offense, but I'm not sucking any of your dicks. I'll choose her over you every damn time."

"Fair enough," Mammoth replied.

"But," I added, giving them each a tick of my chin, "I'm done with those Russian assholes. They've been in Tonopah too damn long. I became a Ghost because I don't like to see innocents suffer when I can prevent it. Ten years in the Corps and combat overseas taught me a hell of a lot about fighting an enemy. You all need my sharpshooter skills, and I won't rest until those girls are safe. Hope I get a chance to fire a bullet between Stepan's eyes too. Maybe we'll get lucky, and his bitch Sergei will be with him."

Rael chuckled, leaning forward to slap me on the back. "Hell fuckin' yeah!"

Mammoth grinned as he turned to Grim. "He's cleared by me, pres."

"Same." Rael stood, his smile fading. "Got shit to take care of, pres. I'll make sure everyone is ready."

"Club is on lockdown until we save those girls. Family stays at the Crossroads. Need everyone ready in an hour," Grim ordered.

The SAA and VP left the three of us alone as Grim sighed, turning to Twitchy. "You want to know about Toad."

"Why isn't he here, Grim?"

"He's laying low. I told him to stay put."

"Laying low? What's he doing? Why?" Twitchy squirmed in my lap, and I held her tighter, forcing her to relax. "What does that mean?"

"Wish I could tell you everything, but I gave my word to a brother," Grim answered, his fists clenching as he refused to give more information.

"That's not how it works. He's a prospect. My cousin hasn't patched in yet."

"I'm aware, Davina."

Her shoulders slumped, and she reached across the table, tapping his clenched fist. "Let me help him. Tell me where he went. If he's in trouble, he shouldn't be alone."

"He's not alone," Grim replied quietly. "Laramie is with him."

Twitchy's hand pulled back, and she cursed, hopping off my lap while throwing her hands in the air. The woman was full of drama, but she sure looked hot as fuck as she strutted around the room.

"You're not going to say anything else, are you?"

"Not my place. You'll have to speak to your cousin. This goes deep, Twitch."

She lowered her head, sniffling a few times before her chin lifted. "Fine. I'll do it later. Right now, I need to keep my head in the game. We've got Russians to fuck up."

Grim smirked. "Damn straight."

Jumping to my feet, I hauled Twitchy into my arms. "We'll figure it out. All of it."

She lifted on her tiptoes and pressed a kiss to my lips. "Thanks."

"I got you," I assured her. "Always."

ROYAL BASTARDS MC

TEN

Twitchy

"DAMN, BABY. IT FEELS good to have you between my legs again," I whispered, running my hand lovingly over my Harley's shiny black paint and chrome. "I promise I won't stay away that long again."

Ace shook his head, but a sweet smile lingered on his lips as he winked. "You ready for this, sweetness?"

Whenever I was about to do something dangerous, I asked myself that same question. Was there a way to be ready? I didn't think so.

Taking a deep breath, I closed my eyes, blocking out the distraction of the other RBMC members and their Harleys, Ace's handsome face, the crisp wind whipping across the desert sands, and the beat of my heart. I let it all fade away and just breathed. The world ceased to exist as the familiar pull on my consciousness brought bright light and warmth even the sun couldn't mimic.

There was no hint of the ugliness of the world to tarnish the beauty I felt, and in my mind's eye, I saw my mother standing in a halo of golden sparkles. She never spoke in a voice that could be called human. I didn't think she was real, a ghost, or even an angel. She simply existed to provide comfort, trust, and genuine affection—a link to whatever gift I had been given and to share in its wondrous knowledge.

Peace descended upon me. A lightness that spread from my core outward until every muscle in my body felt relaxed. Waves of tranquility draped over my head and shoulders, and I knew that whatever happened today would occur exactly as intended. As the feeling began to dim, I held out my hand. My mother grasped it, squeezing it before she smiled. Her presence faded as the golden sparkles disappeared and only the heavy, thick promise of bloodshed remained.

"I'm good." Turning to Ace, I blew him a kiss. "Time to kick some ass."

The pres of the Tonopah chapter sat in the saddle of his Harley, staring me down with a flicker of concern. "Twitchy?"

He knew me well and understood the gravity of what we faced today. I ticked my chin his way. "Ready to ride."

The Royal Bastards owned the Great Basin and had hidden locations throughout the state. They knew everyone, had connections in every major organization, and until recently, the law kept its distance. That was another subject entirely. Point was, the RBMC ruled Nevada. Even the desert wasn't a stranger to men who ruled by violence and Lucifer's curse. It wasn't my secret to tell, but Ace would probably witness shit today he thought was only possible in fiction.

It didn't matter now. Ace made his choices. It was time to focus on the task at hand.

The plan was simple. We knew the stretch of road where Stepan and his Russian goons were supposed to stop the van and capture the girls, but it was miles of open highway on 95.

To keep things as simple as possible, we chose a spot every five mile markers to leave men, branching out across the road in order to ambush the Russians before they could make their move. Plenty of tumbleweed, cactus, and rock kept everyone hidden. The bikes were lowered down on their sides to keep them from view.

It wasn't ideal, but any structures or vehicles would be noticed immediately. The only cage we kept parked on the side of the road was the SUV I borrowed from Grim. Ace hunkered down inside with a rifle and his Glock as I pretended to be stranded, the hood up as I stood in a skimpy, lowcut top. My bike was parked next to the passenger side panel in the dirt closest to the desert, and I hoped it wouldn't arouse suspicion.

It was less than thirty minutes before the estimated time that the girls would leave school for their field trip to Vegas. I tried not to be concerned that I hadn't heard from Inferno or Duchess. They were both coming from long distances, and shit with the club could have stalled their departure.

Ace called out my name as I sighed, leaning against the door as I checked both ways to be sure no vehicles were approaching. Not a soul was on the road, but that would change soon. We risked being stopped by passersby, but that couldn't be helped.

"I'm good. Anxious, bored, worried, maybe," I admitted, noting that he looked just as impatient as I felt.

"We're going to stop them, baby. I know—"

"Shit," I cursed, cutting him off. "There's a big dark van headed this way."

I pretended to be working on the engine as a vehicle approached and then slowed down, stopping on my left.

"You got car trouble?" The voice didn't belong to anyone I'd formally met prior to today, but it made my skin crawl. I recognized his accent from the night I snuck into a similar van, one driven by the two Russian idiots he left behind to clean up his mess.

I lifted my head, staring into the face of none other than Stepan Utkin. The man I'd watched kill two others in cold blood at the high school before he yanked some blonde out the door to use and abuse.

"I'm fine. Waiting on my boyfriend to bring back gas and a tow truck," I lied. The last thing I wanted to do was engage in conversation with a murderer and rapist.

"You sure you don't need any help?"

Hell no. "Nope. Thanks!" I waved, acting like I didn't care if he moved on when I was practically ready to jump out of my skin. *Like I'd walk right up and get in his creepy-rapist-pedophile van.*

"I'll check on you in an hour when I return this way."

I bet he would so that he could pop me into the van with the rest of the girls he kidnapped. "Uh, thanks!" I yelled, waving again as he sped off.

As soon as they were far enough away that my voice couldn't be overheard, I yelled for Ace. His smooth, deep, sultry tone sent shivers down my spine.

"You did good, precious. So fucking proud of you. That was unexpected, but you handled it like a pro. I already texted Grim. He's watching for their van. Gave them the plate, so we're good. You can relax."

Relax? Right.

An incoming call came through on my phone, and I yanked it from my back pocket, relieved to see Rael's name. "Hey."

"We're following the girls. They just left the school."

Good. First part of the plan in place. "Stepan already drove by in a black van. He's going to be waiting for them."

"And we're all waiting on him. Gonna fuckin' love this, Twitchy. My Reaper can't wait to play."

"You know that's creepy as fuck, right? Like super dark and scary?"

A sinister laugh was his only response.

"Ace and I are on the way. Who's out this far besides us?"

"Mammoth and Wraith. They'll let us know if anyone comes back that way."

"Perfect." I hung up, rushing to close the hood of the SUV as Ace slid behind the wheel. I texted Shadow, asking him to pick up my Harley and return it to the Crossroads. An odd feeling swirled in my gut, and I knew I needed to stay in the SUV with Ace. No visions yanked my attention from the present, but I could sense something disastrous looming ahead, and it wasn't the Russians.

We sped along Hwy 95 until we closed in on the traffic, slowing to a more regular speed.

Ace noticed the black van first. "I think we should stay behind those Russian fuckers. I got a weird feeling in the pit of my stomach."

That made two of us. Ace might not have the same heightened senses I did, but he was intuitive. His military skills only sharpened his attention to detail. "Okay. Keep your distance. Try not to make it look like we're tailing them."

"Goddess, you worry too much."

I slapped his arm as he laughed, reaching for my hand and giving it a tender squeeze. "Maybe."

"How're your Spidey senses? Everything kosher?"

"You say the weirdest things," I pointed out, making a face.

"Just checking in, you know? Keeping things real."

"How's this for real? I want to fuck up these Russians, make them suffer, watch as the blood and life oozes from their bodies, then fuck you until I'm no longer coherent."

"Damn, baby. You're goddamn perfect."

"I know," I teased, turning back to the road as Ace frowned. "What is it?"

"What's the name of the high school again? For the girls playing for the volleyball team."

Like there was any other that mattered right now. "Juniper Springs. Ten girls and two chaperones are going to the game today."

"Shit," Ace cursed. "I can see their van. It's about a half-mile ahead of the Russians."

Where the fuck was Rael, Grim, and the rest of the club?

"They're speeding up!" I shouted, nearly ready to panic.

"We have to stop them, babe." Ace pushed his foot down hard on the gas pedal as we lurched forward. "I'm going to ram into the back of their van and slow them down."

"You're going to what?" I screeched, wondering if he was crazy.

"You got a better idea? We can't shoot at them to get their attention with so many other vehicles on the road. There're dozens of people. I might still cause an accident, but at least I won't put a bullet in some kid."

Nodding my head as I swallowed hard, hoping we didn't hurt anyone other than our target, I knew he was right and agreed. "Do it."

Ace pulled up to the van much quicker than I expected. The back doors were shut, and there wasn't a window. They wouldn't notice we'd bumped them until it was too late. He floored the pedal, and we smashed into the back end, causing the van to swish from side to side.

"That wasn't hard enough!"

"I know, sweetness. Trust me. I want their attention. Focusing on us, they won't be able to go after the girls."

Solid plan, right?

He revved the engine and hit the back bumper so hard it detached and flung off to the side, bouncing down the highway out of sight.

The second hit must have pissed them off because the back doors flew open, and guns were pointed in our direction. The black van swerved to avoid another bump as Ace sped up, moving alongside the vehicle on the left. Hwy 95 was only two lanes. He'd have to watch for oncoming traffic.

"That's as close as I'm letting you get. Give them hell!"

My gun was already in my hand, and I leaned out of my window, shooting at the tires to slow the van down. None of them hit where I wanted. Several bullets dented the hood of our SUV as they returned fire, but we managed to match their speed and maintain it.

Ace steered with one hand and shot with his Glock in the other, tapping the trigger fast and with a precision that I was almost envious of. I guess I forgot when he said he was a sharpshooter in the Marine Corps.

A scream caught my attention as the same blonde whore from the high school teetered on the edge of the van's back door. She clung to one of the Russians, who shook his head and shoved her out, laughing as her body flew through the air and landed on the unforgiving asphalt. She wasn't innocent, but she didn't deserve to die. At the speed we were driving, she'd have severe injuries, if not worse.

We couldn't help her, and I hoped someone else would call 9-1-1.

Ace slammed his fist on the windowsill and then lifted his gun, shooting the asshole who pushed her in the forehead. The Russian tumbled out, flopping like a ragdoll on the highway before another trafficker took his place, firing off bullets in rapid succession. One punctured our front tire. We swerved as Ace tried to maintain control.

"Fuck!"

Cars headed in our direction, and Ace yanked the wheel, merging us onto the shoulder. Dirt and sand mingled with rocks as the undercarriage of the SUV sped along, taking damage as Ace struggled not to crash.

I took advantage of the black van's location when we swung to the far left, and I faced the back with the open doors. Stepan appeared and noticed me right away. Our eyes locked as confusion flittered over his features. Everything clicked a second later, and he snarled, lifting his weapon. The bullet left his gun at the exact moment that I fired two shots.

The SUV fishtailed, yanking my body to the right. The whole frame shook as the tire exploded, and I didn't know how Ace managed to keep us from slamming into another vehicle. A single breath left my chest before I noticed what he'd done.

Ace was in the path of Stepan's bullet as it pierced the windshield, followed by his right shoulder before it exited and lodged in the back seat.

"Ace!" I screamed, far too concerned about him to pay attention to the chaos around us.

"Davina, baby, I'll be fine. Clean shot. Bullet went all the way through."

He grunted as the SUV slowed down, and the van spurred on ahead of us, chasing down their target as greed trumped the need to kill us both. The last thing I noticed was the look of triumph on Stepan's face. He would return to finish the job once the girls were in his possession.

Ace blinked while bright red blood soaked through the material of his shirt and dripped onto the upholstery. We slowed considerably as he let his foot off the gas and placed it on the brake, trying to stop us without getting hit by traffic. We swerved onto the median and managed to come to a complete stop without any further damage.

"Gonna need help, goddess." His voice slurred, and I panicked.

"Grady! Don't you die on me! Don't you dare!"

"Not gonna happen, Davina." His head fell back as he coughed. "Kiss me."

My lips lowered to his, and he returned the kiss for a few seconds before his mouth went slack.

Completely freaked out, I began shouting, pleading with God for help. "Don't take him! Please!"

ROYAL BASTARDS MC

ELEVEN

"HOW'S HE DOIN'?"

I looked up at the door, noticing Grim as he leaned against the polished wood. "Better. He's been in and out of consciousness, but I think the worst is over. I don't know what I would have done without Patriot's help."

"He's the best when it comes to bullet wounds. Sure has dug a few out for the club."

"I can imagine."

Grim pushed off the door and sat across from me in an empty chair. "You haven't asked what happened yet."

"No, I haven't," I agreed. Tears misted my eyes for a brief moment before I blinked them back. "I've been too concerned for Ace."

"I get that. If my ol' lady were hurt, I'd be the same way." He cleared his throat before a look of pure menace crossed his features. "We stopped the van before it reached the girls' volleyball team."

"I figured as much. Rael would have moped around the clubhouse for a month if he missed his chance to reap souls."

Grim couldn't hide his humor as he barked out a short laugh. "True enough." He shifted awkwardly in his chair, and I wondered what else was on his mind. "I got Stepan myself. Fucker laughed until my Reaper took his soul."

No surprise there. I hated missing out on that, but Ace needed me, and I wasn't leaving his side. "He got off easy if you ask me."

"I made sure it hurt," he snickered. "All of Stepan's men are dead. Seven souls were sent to Lucifer to enjoy. I don't have to tell you the kind of torment those assholes will endure. Makes my black heart happy to know we saved that group of girls from a terrible fate."

"Me too."

"Resnikov won't get away. We're in a war now, and the Royal Bastards won't stop until every last one of those motherfuckers is sent to Lucifer in hell. Leave it to us. This isn't a worry for the Harlots."

"I don't make that decision, Grim."

"Maybe not, but you have influence. Talk to the Duchess and Inferno. I need this worked out before more trouble comes our way."

"I'll do what I can."

"Good. They're both passed out right now." His lips twitched as if he fought back a smile. "Never met two women more fuckin' crazy in my life." He wasn't wrong. "Stay as long as you like. Ace has proven his worth, and I'd like to offer him a chance to prospect with the club. You're family, Davina. We take care of our own." Grim stood, and I knew the conversation was over.

86

Touched by his words, I nodded. "Thank you, Grim."

He walked across the room, giving me a chin lift before he left and shut the door. The room was silent for several minutes as I thought over his words. I understood what Grim meant, but he wasn't burdened by a promise he needed to fulfill. I wasn't breaking my word. Not to Toad.

"Hey," a deep voice croaked, pulling me from the gloomy space my thoughts occupied, and I gasped, turning to Ace.

"You're awake!"

He groaned, and I started checking his bandages to ensure he wasn't bleeding through the stitches. "Stop. I need a kiss. That's it."

My lips eagerly pressed to his, but I was gentle, afraid I might cause him further pain.

"What the hell was that?" he asked with a grunt.

"Not good enough?"

"Hell no. Rock my world, baby."

I lowered my head and gave him the most passionate, heartfelt, sensual kiss I could muster. When our lips parted, his blue eyes glazed over.

"Son of a bitch. Are you sure I'm not already dead? That was pure heaven."

"No," I giggled, slapping his arm. "Don't think you're getting off that easy. Death would be mercy after I get finished with you."

A smirk settled on his lips. "Oh? What you talkin' about, goddess?"

"You swerving the SUV to take the bullet meant for me."

"Every fuckin' time," he answered vehemently. "Better get used to it."

The playfulness vanished, and I fought back the tears threatening to spill.

"No. Don't you do that again, you hear me? I don't ever want to see you shot and bleeding while I'm helpless to do a goddamn thing."

"It was a clean shot. No big deal."

Grabbing his jaw, I made him look into my eyes. "I thought I was going to lose you," I choked out. "You understand? You're my heart, Grady Barnes."

His features softened as he swallowed hard, reaching for my hand. His fingers closed around mine as he smiled. "I'm stuck with you then, huh?"

"Damn straight. You just kiss me, love me, give me your cock every day, and we should live happily ever after."

Soft laughter rumbled in his chest before he winced. "I think I can live with that."

"Always?"

"Always, precious. Come here."

I lowered my head onto his left shoulder, careful of his wounds as he wrapped an arm around my waist, holding me tight. "Yes, Ace."

"Yes, to what?"

"To marriage. You buy me a stupid, big ass diamond to seal the deal."

"You got it. On one condition."

"What's that?"

"We both get inked. I want my name on your pretty skin, and I can't wait to have you tattooed over my heart."

"You're pretty fucking perfect, Grady."

His grip tightened. "That's why we're so good together, Davina."

"So," Georgia drawled in her southern accent, "when you gonna fill us in?"

"On?" I asked, pouring us each a shot of Fireball as I gave her and my pres Inferno a shrug.

"Don't you play coy with me, honey," she responded, leaning back in her seat as Spook walked by, and she slapped him on the ass. "Grab me a Coke, would ya, darlin'?"

He blushed, scooting around her quickly as he nodded.

"Thanks."

"You know, maybe he doesn't like his ass slapped," Inferno mused. "Kid looked a bit scared."

I snorted, agreeing with her.

"Naw, he's fine."

"How do you know?" I asked, almost immediately regretting the question when she leaned forward, ticking her chin my way.

"He didn't have any complaints when his cock was in my mouth."

"Well, damn," Inferno chortled, slapping the table. "I guess that answers the question of where you spent the night."

"Hell yeah, it does. I have no complaints. Spook took care of me."

Smirking, I tilted my head to the side. "You like 'em young?"

"Thang is, sweet cheeks; I like a guy with stamina. Spook lasted the whole night."

She grinned wide when he returned, handing over the Coke. As their fingers touched, he gently squeezed before releasing her hand. "When I come back to the Crossroads, I want to see you."

"Sure, Georgia. I'd like that."

She tugged him closer, pressing her lips to his. "Don't forget me, handsome."

He appeared dazed. "I won't."

As Spook left us, Georgia opened her Coke, pouring half into her glass before filling the rest with Fireball. She took a sip, finally noticing that Inferno and I watched. "What?"

"He's young," Inferno warned.

"And he's a prospect," I added.

She frowned at both of us. "Why you bustin' my balls? Spook is twenty-two. I'm twenty-eight. Not much of an age difference."

My lips twitched. She was right. I just liked giving her shit. So did Inferno.

My pres leaned back, folding her arms over her chest. "You like him, go for it. I don't give a shit." She bit her lip, and I knew something crazy would pop out of her mouth. "Does he like menage?"

"Fuckkkk," Georgia dragged out, puffing out her tits like it would impress Inferno. "I'm not sharin', pres. His cock is just for me."

The three of us laughed, and I shook my head. Georgia was a curvy, 5'4" blonde with a thick ass and bright smile. She was sweet, pretty, and always used her manners—a true Georgia peach from the south. Not a single Royal Bastard brother had succeeded in taking her to bed until Spook.

"He's a sweetheart."

"And he's a big boy," Inferno added, her gaze roaming over Spook as he slid behind the bar to restock ice.

Spook wasn't fat at all, but he did have a stocky build.

"I like 'em big all over," Georgia deadpanned.

I snorted, flashing her a grin. "I bet you do."

She snickered. "He's got dreamy blue eyes too. And lucky for me, he's only a few hours away when I want a good fuck. I wanna hug and squeeze him and ride his thick rod. Real soon."

Inferno made gagging noises. "Stop. Please. I can't hear that shit."

Laughing, I hid my amusement behind a cough.

"What about you, Twitch? I want to know about Ace."

"Well," I began, sitting up straight, "He's a beast in and out of the sheets."

"Yesssss," Georgia replied, lifting her fist as we bumped knuckles. "Thought so. You got yourself a badass Marine from what I hear."

"Do tell," Inferno added.

"You're never going to believe this, but," I paused, a stupid smile on my face, "I love him."

Georgia's jaw dropped open.

Inferno whistled low, her arms dropping to her sides. "No shit?"

Yeah, it was a big deal. Never said those three words to any other guy, not since I was a teen.

"He's sexy and charming and too goddamn confident, but his cock," I paused again for dramatic effect, "*Wow*."

"Fuck me," Inferno blurted. "Now I'm just jealous."

Georgia giggled, finishing off her drink. "I'm horny now. I'm going to find Spook for a quickie."

Before either of us could respond, she rose to her feet and sauntered toward the door.

"I swear she likes to be shocking."

"Always," I agreed.

"Ace is a lucky guy. He better treat you right."

"If not, I'll kick his ass," I promised.

Inferno nodded. "Good."

I picked up my shot, tossing it back as she leveled me with a hard stare. "I'll pretend I don't see your mothering look, pres."

"You're not fooling anyone, Twitch."

"About?" I asked, pushing the bottle of Fireball away.

"I didn't forget what happened to your cousin or the assholes who tried to kill him."

"They slit his throat," I ground out through clenched teeth. "I'm not letting that slide."

"Is that why you gave your promise in the hospital?"

"He nearly died."

"Yeah, I got you, babe. You know that."

"Yeah," I admitted.

"Then you don't go off doing anything stupid, especially on your own. You hear me?"

"Is that an order, pres?"

"Fuck, Twitchy, don't make it one."

"She won't."

I turned my head, catching the deep, raspy tone of Ace's voice. He must still be in pain because he wobbled slightly before lowering into the chair next to mine.

"We're in this together, goddess."

"You're supposed to be resting," I pointed, not bothering to hide my irritation.

Ace just smiled, not saying another word.

Inferno looked pleased. "There won't be an issue, right, Twitch?"

"Sure," I replied, placing my hand on Ace's arm and patting it lightly. "We're good."

"I GOTTA GO, BABE," Duchess informed me, sitting her ass down on the seat of her bike. "I know it's last minute, but I've got shit going down, and it can't wait."

"We didn't even get a chance to talk," I pointed out, huffing a little with disappointment.

"I know. If it weren't super important, I'd be staying here. At least I know that you all have this handled."

Duchess had been scarce since her arrival, and I wondered what was happening to keep her so distracted. "You sure you're okay?"

"Yeah." She sighed, lifting her slender shoulders in a shrug. "Life, babe. Shit with the club never ends."

"You need help?"

"No, not yet. Besides, you can't leave until you've avenged your cousin. Don't think Inferno didn't say anything. She did."

I didn't try to hide it. "Am I just supposed to be okay with it? Act like nothing happened?"

"No, Twitchy. I can feel your pain." She reached out her hand, squeezing once as her glove wrapped around my fingers. "I love you. You know that. Just promise me you'll stay safe. Be smart about it."

"Yeah, okay."

"Trust those super sensitive senses of yours, and don't get hurt."

"I'll do my best," I promised, squeezing her hand back. Safe travels."

"Later, babe. I'll be in touch."

I watched her roll out of the Crossroads lot, Paramore and Roulette flanking her on the left and right. As I stood there, I thought about my conversation with both of the women I admired most in my life. Neither was wrong to approach me. We were family. Looking out for one another was part of our code. It went farther than that too. As women, we faced obstacles, stigma, and enemies our male friends never had to worry about. Facing those hardships sealed a bond of sisterhood that combined with the familial loyalty and camaraderie we felt in the Royal Bastards MC. As Harlots, we earned a place by their side.

Warmth blossomed in my chest. Yeah, family wasn't always those you shared blood with.

ROYAL BASTARDS MC

TWELVE

Ace

"IT'S NOT YOUR CALL to make, Twitchy."

"Grim. This is my cousin we're talkin' about. My family."

"Aren't we family too?"

Blinking, I opened my eyes, catching part of the argument I could hear between Twitchy and the president of the Royal Bastards. Neither was doing a sufficient job of keeping their voices down. My feisty goddess stood in the doorway, directly across from me. Her back faced my direction, making her unaware that I'd roused.

"Of course. We're bonded by brotherhood."

"Then what's the problem with letting us handle Resnikov? Those fucking Russians deal currency in human flesh. You aren't invincible. Reapers are, Twitch."

Reapers?

I'd heard talk of them on more than one occasion, but I wasn't sure why the Tonopah chapter referred to themselves that way. Was it their brutality? I didn't know, and it was the least of my worries.

My shoulder throbbed as I winced. The stabbing ache had receded to a consistent painful pulse that snatched my breath whenever I moved around too much. I'd been shot before, so it wasn't like I couldn't handle it, but that was in the past, along with the years I spent overseas. Shit I didn't like to think about now that I retired.

My body felt sore and unused, stiff like I hadn't gotten out of bed in weeks. I hated that feeling. This sucked balls. I was an active guy, worked out nearly every day, and I kept in top physical condition. After so many years in the Corps, it was routine. PT was a way of life like chow three times a day and cleaning my weapons.

Sighing softly, I continued to listen to Twitchy, wondering what was going on in her pretty head. When she finished the conversation with Grim and turned around, I could see the fatigue on her face. Instead of asking a bunch of questions, I held out my hand. She didn't hesitate to walk toward me, sinking onto the bed as I tugged her closer with my good arm. It still jostled me a bit, but I didn't complain.

"Close your eyes, precious. Let's take a nap."

I thought she would refuse or struggle to let the shit she discussed with Grim go, but she snuggled against my side. She closed her eyes with one arm wrapped around my waist and her cheek over my heart.

"Ace?"

"Yeah, sweetness?"

She paused, taking a couple of breaths. "Thank you."

"For what?"

"Being you."

A light chuckle escaped my lips. "I'm all yours, baby."

I held her for several hours, dozing off and on as Davina slept. During that short time, I felt contentment that I never knew before we met. She completed me, as silly as that was, and I hoped she'd stick around for a long time. I wasn't needy. Hell, I was about as independent as any guy could get. I'd seen and done shit most men would never experience as a Marine. But Davina? She rocked my world, and I didn't want to let her go.

"Got you, my sweet," I whispered, tightening my embrace briefly. "Always."

"HOP IN THE CAR," Twitchy ordered, opening the driver's side door of the SUV she "borrowed" from Grim again. An hour ago, we snagged a bit to eat after our nap. She squirmed in her seat the entire time, and I noticed the faraway look in her eyes. My girl was restless.

Time to figure out what she needed and how to give it to her, preferably while we worked out all the details as I fucked her. Sure, that sounded crass, but I was goddamn addicted to her pussy and not afraid to admit it.

"Where are we goin'?" I asked, parking my ass on the passenger seat.

"There's not enough privacy at the Crossroads. We need a distraction."

A distraction? "You're not concerned about Resnikov?"

"Yeah, but what am I going to do about it, huh?" She blew out a frustrated breath, hitting the steering wheel with her palm.

"Hey," I chided. "What's going on? You can talk to me," I reminded her gently.

"I know, Ace."

"Then what's bugging you?"

"I hate it when I'm not in control," she admitted, making a face. "Seriously, we rescue those girls and take out a few of the traffickers, but Resnikov gets away, and there isn't shit we can do about it? We just sit around waiting for him to make another move? I don't like it."

"Yeah, I feel you, precious. It's shit. Not gonna lie."

"Then you understand how restless I feel."

"Sure do. You think Marines aren't familiar with patience? Fuck. The motto of the Corps is hurry up and wait. Drives you fucking nutty."

She smirked. "I bet."

"But that's life, beautiful," I reminded her. "We can't control anything but ourselves."

"Yeah, I guess you're right."

"Say that again."

"Oh, shut it," she laughed. "I'm confident enough in my womanhood. I can admit my man knows his shit."

"Why, thank you, darlin'," I rasped in my best southern accent.

Twitchy giggled. "Thanks. I needed that."

"I know everything you need, goddess. Let's find a place to crash, and I'll show you."

"You know what? I'm going to take you up on that."

"Do it," I groaned, my cock stiffening as I imagined all the ways I'd fuck her soon.

"Damn, Ace. Stop staring at me like that before I pull over and we fuck in the SUV."

"Who said we can't?" I asked with a wicked grin.

"Your shoulder," she pointed out, giving me a stern look. "We should be careful."

"Did I say I wanted careful? Hell no, baby. You pull over and ride my cock. Right fucking now."

Not giving her a chance to argue, I unzipped my jeans, taking out my dick. She glanced my way, biting her bottom lip as I began to stroke the length, hissing as my hips bucked.

"Ace."

"No, my goddess."

She groaned, pulling off the road. The tint was fairly dark on the SUV, but that didn't mean people couldn't see us if they looked close enough. I didn't care. Let them look.

"The backseat has more room," she announced, opening her door and sliding off the seat.

I followed her, scrambling to keep my jeans up as I joined her. My ass planted down as she helped me strip off my clothes, leaving my shirt since lifting my arm would have been nearly impossible. Bandaged up, I could move a little, but anything more with that shoulder would probably cause me to pass out from the pain.

I ignored the ache all the movement was causing, focusing on the sexy, naked woman who straddled me. Her thighs rested on the seat on either side of my hips. My gaze focused on her pussy, staring at the vee between her legs with undisguised hunger.

"Are you wet for me?" I asked in a gravelly tone, lifting my hand to brush across her folds, sliding through the slit with my fingers. I probed the smooth, silky skin and then slid two fingers inside her tight cunt, gently thrusting in and out.

Her breath hitched in her throat as Davina's head tilted back. Her hands gripped my shoulders as her hips slowly began to rock.

"Is this what you need?" I asked huskily, growling when her cunny dripped onto my fingers.

"Ace."

"Tell me," I ordered, "Describe what you want in detail."

"Keep pumping your fingers and—"

A squeal left her lips, cutting off her words when I pressed down on her clit, rubbing it while I kept up the pace. A lascivious grin spread across my face when I heard the greedy sucking sounds her pussy made.

My fingers pulled out as she gasped, and I licked them, making eye contact. "So fucking delicious."

"Ace."

I shook my head. She didn't get it. I wanted to hear my real name. No, I needed her to scream my real name as I fucked her hard.

My hands reached for her hips, pulling her down on my lap. Her tits pressed against my chest as she grasped my erection, giving a couple of deep tugs. "Shit," I groaned, impatient to feel her pussy gripping my dick.

Her carnal smile proved she knew exactly how to tease me. She lifted on her knees, lining up my dick. Without a word, she began feeding the tip inside her cunt.

It took all my focus not to ram up inside her, taking all the control. Sweat dripped down the side of my face as I stared into her eyes, waiting for her to continue.

Three heartbeats passed while neither of us moved, and then Davina began pistoning her body, slowly raising higher and lowering her knees, every plunge taking a little bit more of my cock and feeding it into her channel. *So fucking wet. So goddamn tight.* I gripped her hips, unable to resist.

And then we both wrestled for control.

Davina's head tilted back as she moaned, riding my cock while I bounced her up and down on my dick.

Every stroke caused both pain and pleasure. My body couldn't decide which was more important. I hissed as the pain in my shoulder intensified, combined with the intense way her pussy hugged my cock. *So fucking good.*

"Play with your clit," I ordered, watching as she slid a hand down her stomach, teasing the sensitive bundle of nerves.

I watched her, learning the speed and rhythm she liked. I'd do it for her next time, watching her fall apart beneath me. Probably while I licked and fucked her cunt with my mouth.

Fuck. I was so turned on that I could hardly focus on anything but all the dirty ways I wanted to fuck her in the future. My hips rolled as I kept thrusting, fucking her as small moans filled the cab of the SUV. Her walls fluttered around my dick, and I knew she would come soon.

"Give it to me, Davina. Fucking soak me. I want to feel you choke my dick as you come."

Her eyes flashed with desire as I grasped her ass and plunged deeper, filling her to the base as one of her hands gripped my good shoulder.

The other kept beating her clit, the fingers moving fast as she rocked her hips. I could feel the exact moment she came. Her pussy clenched my dick so hard I growled, followed by the flood of her release. She gushed over us both, dripping down my cock and over my balls, turning me on even more.

"Grady!"

There. She said it.

With strength I didn't know I had, I had her on her back on the seat, fucking her hard through her orgasm. My entire body felt engulfed in flames, both pleasure, and pain, and I couldn't hold back a second longer, flooding her pussy with my cum.

"Davina, fuck!" I roared, slamming inside her a few more times before I collapsed, my head full of fog and my body spent.

We breathed together, clutching one another close as I lifted my head, capturing her lips in a smoldering kiss. When we parted, I caught the sweet, well-fucked, contented look on her face.

"You're addicting, Grady Barnes."

"Is that only because I fuck you better than anyone else you've ever been with?" I asked, cocky as fuck.

She lifted a hand and cradled my face. "I can't deny it."

"Fucking love you, baby," I replied vehemently.

"Damn straight you do."

"What's the plan, beautiful?"

"We're finding a place to crash. I need some space from the Crossroads."

At that moment, it occurred to me that Davina never took me to her place. I hadn't offered to go to mine yet either, so I opened my mouth, asking if she wanted to go to my place.

"Sure. Let's go."

The drive to my house took only fifteen minutes. I had a spacious three-bedroom home with an attached garage on one of those streets full of families, low crime, and pretty yards full of flowers. It wasn't anything that stood out with beige stucco walls and dark wood trim. I had a wraparound porch, a deck in the back with a grill, lots of furniture to sit on, and a firepit I used year-round.

Twitchy eyed the exterior and gave me a wistful smile. "It's a nice place, Ace."

"Yeah? Move in." I wasn't fucking joking.

"I'll think about it." The way she said it, I wasn't sure if she meant that or not. Davina loved her independence, maybe too much to ever consider living with me. I'd be patient. Someday she'd change her mind.

"Come on. I've got cold beer in the fridge, and I'm thirsty."

She followed me in as I unlocked the front door, sinking onto the couch as I handed her one of the beers. "Thanks."

The rest of the afternoon things felt a little off, but I ignored it, spending time with Davina as we watched a few movies. I might have thought we weren't good after the sex in the SUV, but she rested her head on my shoulder, and I convinced myself everything was okay.

Should have paid attention to my gut.

Sometime in the late evening, we both dozed off. My wound zapped my strength after I overdid it, fucking Davina the way I did. I was exhausted. My body focused on healing, which was why I never heard her leave. Usually, I slept light and noticed the slightest sounds. Tonight I slept so soundly it was almost scary.

Hours later, my eyes snapped open, realizing I was alone. My stomach clenched, and I knew in my gut what had happened. I should have guessed sooner. It was right in front of me from the moment we left the Crossroads.

Fuck.

My goddess was gone.

I didn't have an issue with the fact that she needed space. I just worried she wasn't coming back.

ROYAL BASTARDS MC

THIRTEEN

Twitchy

My cousin Toad had a place in Goldfield. I knew the secret location, a trailer he purchased on his own, and few people knew about it. He called the bit of land he owned his sanctuary.

I understood why he needed the space. Restless souls, we shared the need for the open road, freedom, and at times, privacy. We were a lot alike, and I knew if he brought Laramie here, there was trouble. The entire situation brought me back to the reason I hunted those fucking Russians and the Scorpions MC to begin with—they hurt my family. To be specific, my cousin Ronin. He was more than that to me. We were as close as siblings.

So when I did a little digging after Ace fell asleep, searching through my phone and talking to a few trusted contacts, I realized Ronin's girl was listed on a hit list.

Resnikov wanted her, assumably to add to his trafficking ring if not for his own pleasure first. The sick fuck. I knew I had to get to Ronin and Laramie and bring them to the Crossroads. His place wasn't secure enough. If the Black Market Railroad or the Scorpions MC found them, they'd kill my cousin and take Laramie.

I couldn't allow that.

My head turned as I clicked off my phone, staring at Ace as he slept. His breathing was calm and deep as he faced my direction, his hand on my thigh. My heart thumped hard in my chest when I thought about how fast and hard I fell for this Marine. He was my definition of a perfect man. If you asked me to put together all my preferred characteristics along with a physical description, you'd have my Ace.

I leaned down, pressing my lips to his in a feather-soft kiss. "I'm sorry I'm ditching you," I whispered, pulling away. "But you're already injured, and I'm not letting you take on all the assholes of the world for me when you've already been shot once. I'll come back, Grady. I promise."

I stood, making my way toward his front door. At the last second, I turned around, smiling as he whispered my name in his sleep.

"I love you."

The drive to Goldfield didn't take long. There wasn't much traffic on the road, and I heaved a sigh of relief when I arrived and nothing seemed out of place on Ronin's property.

My cousin's trailer was dark inside. No lights. I didn't worry since it was early, and he likely didn't wake up yet. Probably spent the night in bed with Laramie, which caused my smile to widen. About time he stopped denying what we all knew. Ronin loved Laramie.

I banged on the door, snickering when I could hear him cursing and stumbling around inside. Just to be a pain in the ass, I pounded on the door again.

It swung open, Ronin staring me down. "What the fuck?"

"Ro, I've got to talk to you! It's about Lar—"

"She's here." He tugged Lara closer and wrapped both arms around Laramie from behind. I doubted a crowbar could have pried them loose. "Relax. Calm down the crazy." Ronin kissed the top of her head, and I didn't miss the tenderness in his embrace.

"Well, shit." My head tilted to the side, a snicker releasing from my lips. "It's about damn time. Thought you were never gonna make a move, Ro."

"Right?" Lara asked, giggling. "He took forever."

"Yeah, he did. Stubborn asshole," I agreed. "Let me in. The sun is tryin' to fry my ass out here."

Ronin snorted, shuffling to the side slightly but not releasing his girl.

I rushed inside and slammed the door, flipping the lock before I dropped into a nearby chair. Sighing, he followed me to the dining room table, pulled out a chair, and reached for Lara. She settled on his lap and lay her head on his shoulder.

"This is a bit surreal," I commented, watching as Ronin brushed his hand up and down Lara's back. "I'm glad to see you got your head outta your ass."

He snorted, mildly amused. "What's so important that you're banging down my door like a freak?"

Back to business, I sat forward, propping my elbows on my knees. "Heard some serious shit about, uh, fuck," I cursed, my gaze darting to Laramie. "I don't want to say too much."

"In front of Lara, right?"

"Yeah."

"Hey, I'm not helpless." Laramie sat up, lifting her chin. "I already know more than you think. If this is about the Scorpions, then I think I deserve the truth."

I couldn't help giving her a doubtful look.

"I'm serious. They killed my brother, remember? And yesterday they attacked me in a restaurant. Ronin saved my life."

"Aw, fuck. This is bad. So, so bad."

Ronin tensed. "What is it?" he asked warily, worried as he instinctively pulled Lara back against his chest.

"The Scorpions are linked to the Black Market Railroad. You understand what I'm sayin', Ro? They want her for a fucking auction."

"What!?" Ronin exploded, nearly toppling Lara over as he jumped to his feet. "You need to be sure, Davina. I fucking mean it."

Using my real name made an impact.

I swallowed hard, rising to my feet. "I'm certain. There have been rumors circulating underground. My contact said he heard about a girl matching Lara's description. Mentioned how she lost a brother two years ago and the Scorpions needed to tie up loose ends."

My cousin looked ready to lose his shit. "Fuck."

"It's not just her that's in danger. They want you dead, Ro."

I swallowed hard, trying not to cry. I never even mentioned this to Ace. I didn't want to drag him into this. The less Ace knew, the better.

"I can't protect you alone. Dad's already looking into some of his Ghosts for extra muscle, but we can't be everywhere at once, and we can't compromise Hope's Refuge."

"No," he agreed, "I understand."

"You need to get to the Crossroads as soon as you can. Fill Grim in on all this shit. It's his club in the middle of it and his personal vendetta."

His jaw clenched. "I'll tell Grim everything."

"But he won't share it all with you. Not until you patch in. Tell him you're ready. Make Diablo speak up for you. He's your sponsor. With the whole club backing you up, you've got a chance to handle what needs to be done."

"Kill them all," Ronin whispered as Laramie gasped.

"It's the only way," I replied firmly. "I'll come with you to the Crossroads, but then I've got some shit to take care of, and it can't wait." As soon as these two were dropped off and safe, I'd keep my promise and take care of those assholes.

"Don't tell me you're going after these motherfuckers alone."

"Hell no, I've got backup." *Yeah, sure.*

"That's not funny," he snapped, giving me a look like he knew what I planned.

"I'll be careful, Ro. I promise. Pack a bag. We need to ditch this place as soon as possible."

"And my bike?"

"I've got it covered."

"THERE'S A LOT TO this story," Ronin was saying as he held Laramie in his lap, facing his MC brothers.

Grim ushered us inside after we arrived, gathering the members in the chapel. The doors shut behind us as everyone sat at the end of a long, polished oak table. In the center, etched into the wood, was the club's insignia—a skull wearing a crown with twin motorcycles exploding from the left and right.

A dozen chairs were occupied around the perimeter, each man staring at Ronin as he began his tale.

I was the only one standing as I leaned against the wall, offering an encouraging smile when he glanced my way. It was time Grim learned the truth from Ronin. No more secrets.

"Need every single detail, son," Grim replied.

"Don't leave nothin' out," Rael added.

"He won't," Diablo announced, squeezing Ronin's shoulder. "Toad ain't fucking around now that he's got his ol' lady. Are you?"

"No," Ronin confirmed, shaking his head. "Probably should have said this shit a long time ago. I just didn't know how."

A few nods followed around the table like they understood what he meant.

"Most of you know I had shit parents. My old man left my mom when I was a baby, and she was a drunk who let me starve and run around dirty. When I met Laramie's parents, I was underweight and probably would have ended up in the foster care system within six months."

I hated this part of the story. It was the only part of Ronin's life I wasn't involved in.

"Blake and I were the same age and had the same interests. We were wild boys. Got into everything and never could sit still. When we discovered dirt bikes and motorcycles, everything changed. It gave us something to do, and we loved it."

More nods accompanied those words.

"And then I started noticing other things, particularly girls."

Knowing smirks decorated faces all around the table. One of the guys, Shadow, bumped fists with Ronin.

"Laramie was the one who stole my heart. Never was any other girl but her," he admitted, leaning down to kiss the top of her head, "and it scared the fuck out of me, so I tried to run from it for a long time."

"I hear you, kid," Diablo replied as Ronin paused briefly.

"Blake was a hothead. He loved everything fast—girls, bikes, weed, parties. We ran wild, and that's when he met Ginny." Ronin's voice turned cold as he swallowed hard.

Ginny was the redheaded bitch who used Blake. *Fuck her.*

"She was bad news. I tried to tell Blake and convince him to walk away, but he begged me to prospect for the Scorpions, so we did."

Rael shook his head. "Damn."

Mammoth, the VP, folded his arms across his chest. "How long you prospect for them?"

"Only a few months. Never made it longer than that because Ginny betrayed Blake. She set him up."

Grim sighed. "Tell us the rest."

"Blake fell hard for that redhead. He worshipped the ground she walked on. He would have done anything for her, so he was shocked when he found out she was the ol' lady for one of the members. Ripper didn't take it well."

"Ripper?" Rael tilted his head to the side. "That fucker is on my shit list too."

"The whole damn club is on your shit list," Mammoth deadpanned as a few chuckles followed.

Ronin inhaled a deep breath as I stiffened, knowing what was coming. Laramie slipped from his grasp, walking toward me as I held out my arms, giving her a hug.

"Blake panicked when Ripper called his cell. He hung up on Blake as he tried to explain he didn't know Ginny was cheating. He truly didn't."

"Love blinded him, I guess. He freaked out, shouting that he was going to leave town and try to escape Ripper's wrath. He asked me to watch over Laramie. That he knew what we meant to one another."

Laramie turned abruptly at his words. "Blake said that?"

"Yeah, baby."

She rushed into his arms as he stood, enveloping me in his embrace.

"The Scorpions arrived before he could leave. A dozen of those motherfuckers attacked us on our front lawn. Ripper shot," he paused, cursing under his breath. "He shot Blake twice at close range. There wasn't shit I could do to save him."

The pain in his voice was too much as he croaked, making a funny sound in his throat, and I hated what they did to him. His scars were soul deep, and I needed retribution for his suffering.

Laramie tried to soothe him. "It wasn't your fault."

He nodded, trying hard to maintain his composure. "That's when the attack happened that I didn't anticipate. The knife that sliced across my throat as they left us both for dead, bleeding out into the fucking grass like a couple of worthless animals."

Diablo and Rael both rose from their seats, each man almost vibrating with anger.

"You were only kids," Rael spat, clearly pissed.

"Fucking hell, son," Diablo cursed, rushing toward Ronin as their foreheads touched briefly. "I got you, brother. I fucking got you. I sponsored you because I knew you had what it takes to be royal. And you proved it more than once."

A few others added their agreement.

No one noticed my anger or the fists that I closed next to my hips, promising vengeance.

Grim rose from his chair, banging a skull-shaped gavel onto the table's wooden surface. "Got a vote to make, my brothers. All those in favor of patchin' in Toad, say aye."

Every single one of them answered.

"All those opposed, say nay."

No one said a word.

"Then we're havin' a little party tonight, my fellow Bastards. Because tomorrow," he sneered, ticking his head toward Ronin. "We're planning how to deal with those assholes permanently."

Not gonna be fast enough, I mused silently.

"Good. I'm needin' a drink, my Nylah, and a whole lot of fuckin' to prepare," Rael announced and then howled up at the roof like a wolf.

Chuckles erupted around us as the doors of the chapel opened.

Mammoth called out to the bar, yelling for shots. Drinks were placed in multiple hands until the room went quiet.

"To our newest patch. Our brother Toad," Grim announced.

Glasses were slammed down after empty, repeatedly filling as the festive atmosphere swirled around us. Ronin was pulled away as I linked arms with Laramie.

"They're going to have a lot of shit to cover with him for a bit. Don't worry. It's all part of the initiation into the club," I assured her.

Diablo was already setting up equipment at a table, instructing Ronin to remove his shirt and have a seat. Rael shoved a bottle of whiskey in his face and told him to take a few lengthy swigs of the liquor.

"Why do they call him Toad? That seems so cruel," Laramie asked, practically yelling to be heard over the shouting, music, and the low thrum of the machine Diablo was using.

"It's a road name. Believe it or not, It's a respect and honor kind of thing. He's been a prospect for over a year and proved his worth, loyalty, and dedication to the club. It means he's accepted, faults and all."

"But they gave him the name before he patched in."

"Yes, they did. Diablo believed in him. He wasn't wrong about my cousin. Ronin is a Royal Bastard through and through. He was born for this." The pride in my voice was unmistakable.

Ronin was Royal. Didn't matter if it was Bastards or Harlots. He was family.

"Yeah, I think you're right."

A fierce sense of belonging and friendship vibrated throughout the room. A brotherhood that went far beyond a love for motorcycles. They clasped each other on the back, told stories, drank a ton, smoked even more, and joked for hours. Beyond that, there was a sincere affection for each brother. This club was a haven, a place to call home. Family.

That was why I knew what had to be done.

ROYAL BASTARDS MC

FOURTEEN

Ace

T WO DAYS. TWO WHOLE fucking days since Davina left.

Pacing the living room in my house, I tried not to get pissed. She ignored every fucking call and text I sent her, and if I wasn't secure in the way she felt about me, I'd be fucking worried. The facts weren't adding up, though. Davina was hiding something from me, and if I had to guess, I'd say it was about those fucking Russians and her family. Not just the Harlots or the Bastards.

I knew her cousin was a prospect, but I hadn't met him yet. He wasn't there the only time I walked inside the Crossroads. But I had a feeling he'd be there now, and I needed his help. Maybe Toad kept in contact with Twitchy and knew where the hell to find my woman. It was worth a shot.

I rode my Harley over to the Crossroads, and luckily the prospect at the gate recognized me from the last time I was there.

"You're Ace, right?"

"Yep. Got some business with Grim about Twitchy."

"Ride on in, man."

Parking in a rush, I barely had the kickstand down before I rushed inside, catching Grim's eyes as he stood, walking away from the bar. Before we could speak, a young man with the same smile and dark hair approached. A hideous scar stretched across his neck, and I knew whatever he'd been through was some serious shit. No wonder Davina felt protective over him. The kid was fucking scarred. Someone slashed his throat. I bet it was the goddamn Scorpions MC.

"Where is she?" he demanded, knowing this was about Davina.

"Name's Ace," I responded, running a hand through my hair in agitation, knowing if Toad hadn't heard from her, it was bad. "I think Twitchy got mixed up in some bad business. I can't find her, and I can't get ahold of her. She's off the grid." I swallowed hard, keeping a tight lid on my simmering temper. "I'm worried she went rogue."

As a Royal Harlot, she was lethal. Twitchy had a wild side, and it was one of the things that I loved about her. She was independent and opinionated and did whatever the fuck she wanted. I just hoped she could stay safe and unharmed until we found her.

"Toad," he gruffly replied. "Her family."

"Yeah, I see the resemblance."

"You sure she's missing?" Toad asked, cracking his knuckles. He seemed frustrated, and I couldn't deny I felt the same way.

"Yeah, Toad. She would have texted me back. I'm guessing you can't get ahold of her either."

"No." He hung his head, breathing a few times before he lifted his chin. "Well, Ace, we need to figure out a plan because we're going to find her."

"I hear ya, kid."

"Good," he snarled, turning to Grim. "Pres, we got a problem."

"What do you want to do, Toad?" Grim stood in front of him as I noticed the room had gone quiet. "She went after the motherfuckers that slit your throat. She's been waiting a long time for vengeance."

"Fuck!" he roared, stomping toward Grim. "We need to help her. I can't let Twitchy go out there alone. She's strong and fierce, but this isn't her fight. It's *mine*," he vehemently argued.

Grim sighed. "Yeah, I know. Twitchy always does whatever the fuck she wants. All the Harlots do." He pinched the bridge of his nose. "Christ," he muttered. "Okay. Let's come up with a plan. We'll hold church and discuss it."

Discuss it? That wasn't good enough. Twitchy was a Harlot. They owed her, and I almost opened my mouth when Toad beat me to it.

"Let me ride with a few of my brothers and Ace. I'll find her," he promised.

"Not gonna happen," Grim announced, staring him down. "You ain't goin' out there, son. Not right now. Those assholes put a hit on you. It's open season when you leave the protection of the Crossroads. I can't allow it until we're ready."

"I can't either," a soft voice added.

Toad turned to Laramie, sighing when he saw the fear in her eyes. "Baby."

"He's right. You can't go."

"She's gonna get killed," he replied in agony.

"No, she isn't, Toad. I'm going after her right now. I'm just here to see what backup I can get."

I ticked my head at Grim.

"I'm a Marine. I know my shit. Who can you send to help? I only need a couple of guys. The rest should stay here to protect the Crossroads."

Grim blew out a breath, clearly agitated, but I didn't know which of the bullshit circumstances going on around us factored into his mood. Maybe all of them at once. Being the club president put him in a position I'd never want to be in.

"Wraith and Patriot. Go with Ace. Find Twitchy and bring her ass back here. We need to talk."

THREE HOURS LATER AND I still didn't have my woman.

All I had in my hands was Davina's phone or what remained of it. We found it outside the Scorpion MC compound. The device was broken into several pieces, and the screen was smashed, but I still recognized it. The Royal Harlots logo was etched into the case.

My shoulders rolled back, and I narrowed my eyes. "I'm going in."

I pushed through Patriot and Wraith, not giving two shits if they tried to stop me. Davina would never smash her phone like this or carelessly leave it for someone else to find.

"Wait." Patriot held up his hands as he jumped in front of me, knowing I didn't want to deal with any more delays. "Hey, I get it. I know you want to rush in there and kick ass. That's what we do."

Fuck yeah. From one Marine to another. We knew our shit. "Then why are you standing in my way?"

"Because if you go in there and start shooting, you're gonna die. Maybe get Twitchy killed too," Wraith explained. "The three of us aren't enough. We need to take this back to Grim."

"What the fuck is he gonna do?" I asked, practically growling the words. "I'm not lettin' anything happen to my woman. Davina could be hurt right now. Who fucking knows what they'll do to her."

"That's why we go back to Grim and grab a few of our brothers. Take the fight to these assholes and fuck up this place."

So, here I was, stomping toward the door of the Crossroads as Patriot and Wraith followed. I didn't wait for them, marching inside as I hollered for Grim. A few heads turned my way. Fuck protocol. Davina was in trouble.

"I'm too old for this shit," Grim complained, staring me down. "You didn't find Twitch?"

"No. Not exactly," I replied.

"What the fuck does that mean?"

"They got her, pres. I think she spotted Ripper at their compound and decided to confront him. Ace found her cellphone smashed outside the gates," Wraith explained.

"She's in there, pres," Patriot added. "We need to move fast."

"Fuck!" I shouted, pacing the common room as I stepped over debris. "You're fucking lucky I didn't rush in there, Grim. I sure wanted to. Wraith and Patriot held me back, but we need to move *now*."

Grim snarled, rushing forward as he got in my face, just inches from touching. "This is my fucking club. You hear me? Don't come in here and act like you can run shit. I won't hesitate to take your ass down, feel me?"

I didn't flinch or move a muscle. My jaw flexed as I sneered. "Yeah, I *feel* you, Grim. So help me get Twitchy back, or I'm doing this shit rogue."

Grim cracked his neck, and I could tell he was about to lose it.

"Hey, Ace," Toad intervened, glancing at Grim before he continued. "There's protocol. We'll help. You think I'm not comin' and ready to put a world of hurt on Ripper? I've been waitin' two fucking years for this. We're gettin' my cousin back. *Chill the fuck out.*"

I almost punched him in the face until I realized my rage was pushing me into a dark place. I took a few breaths, calming enough to see reason. I was leaving in less than a minute and taking back Davina. With or without the Royal Bastards. "Not waiting any longer, Toad."

"I know. Me either." He walked my way, pausing to look back at Grim.

The big dark Bastard nodded, ticking his chin in my direction. "Let's roll out."

ROYAL BASTARDS MC

FIFTEEN

T HE SCORPION MC COMPOUND was quiet tonight. No wild parties or screams coming from the interior. No vans full of trafficked girls. I didn't see any of the Russian boss's vans or any hint they were here.

Well, shit.

Was I wrong? Was Ripper somewhere else?

The Scorpions MC was similar to the Royal Bastards, with many chapters and multiple clubhouses. The Tonopah chapter had three separate locations they used for various purposes. I could be wrong that he preferred this one. Hey, I wasn't always perfect but I sure made that shit look good.

My Spidey senses were tingling a hell of a lot tonight so even if I didn't see Ripper, it didn't mean he wasn't involved in something horrid inside. The Scorpion biker was a menace and the sooner I dealt justice, the better for society.

Crouching low to the ground, I slowly made my way around the perimeter. Several prospects walked along the fence, and I kept quiet, not wanting to attract unnecessary attention. They didn't seem to be concerned, joking around and barely aware of their surroundings. Sloppy.

Shaking my head, I kept moving, watching the compound for any confirmation of Ripper's presence. Hell, if the ones on patrol mentioned him, I'd be happy to learn any intel.

Cameras rolled at specific intervals above the fence tops, ready to catch anyone sneaking up on their location. I'd done plenty of surveillance over the three years since Toad's attack. Ripper was one crafty sonofabitch. He seemed to know I watched and waited for the opportunity to strike. Why he never bothered to confront me was a mystery.

Frustrated, I wasn't wasting any more time. Now that Ronin had Laramie and she was safe, I needed to know the asshole who nearly killed him couldn't come back and try to finish the job. I'd had way too many nightmares about it.

A branch snapped on the ground behind me, and I turned, sucking in a breath.

"Hello, Twitchy."

Fuck. My gun pointed at his head. "Ripper."

He lifted his hand, striking me over the head with the butt of his gun before I could react.

Lights out, dummy, I thought. I shouldn't have come alone.

SOMETIME LATER, A BUZZING sound in my ears slowly brought the present back into focus.

Groaning, I opened my eyes, blinking a few times.

Awareness was slow to creep in, but when it did, the horror of my circumstances began to sink in.

My body was strapped to a wooden cross. The cool surface of the wood stuck to my exposed skin. Tightly lashed against the frame, I couldn't move. My arms and legs were spread open as Ripper stood before me with a cat o' nine tails. Staring down, I noticed I didn't have any clothing covering my body.

I'd been stripped naked.

Fear snaked its way along my spine as my jaw locked. I fought hard against the restraints, trying to loosen the leather straps. Nothing happened. My fingers and toes wiggled, a slight tingling sensation pulsing through my extremities.

Ripper flicked his wrist, whipping his weapon through the air with precision, and fire erupted across my skin.

A bloodcurdling scream launched from my lips.

"You should have known better, little Harlot. Now, you will suffer."

I couldn't respond. Couldn't move. Hell, it hurt to draw a breath into my lungs.

Everything burned where the lash had struck.

He didn't hesitate or make demands. Ripper wasn't interested in anything but my torment. Hours and hours of the same. I had no idea how long he kept me here, strapped down naked and without food or water. My mind rebelled when the pain became too much, and I stopped wishing for anyone to find me—even Ace.

Why was I so fucking stupid?

The day reached night, and I knew it was the last hours I'd live before he finished me off. Ripper seemed to grow bored when I stopped reacting to his taunts. I hardly flinched anymore. My muscles spasmed but only because of the pain and the crack that preceded every single flick of his wrist.

"Tell me Twitchy," he snarled, getting in my face as he forced my head up by cruelly gripping my hair. "When do you think I should fuck you? When the blood is drained from your body? Or when your last few breaths are breaking free from your weak lungs?"

I barely noticed the pool of blood on the floor or the splatters that streaked the walls. Droplets landed on the cross, blending into the wood that was nearly the same color as my skin. Glaring at him in defiance, I refused to comment.

"You bitch—" he began, then paused.

When a commotion reached my ears from outside, I didn't want to believe it. Rescue? Not fathomable. What if I imagined it?

Ripper cursed, hearing the same chaos.

"They're here!" I announced, unsure if it was true, laughing as Ripper dropped the cat o' nine tails, pulling a large knife from his cut. He slid across the side of my face with the blade.

"I'll take you apart piece by piece. They won't find a fucking part of you that's untouched."

"I doubt you'll succeed. You're a dead man," I goaded.

A few Scorpions MC members ran down the stairs, one of them yelling at my captor.

"Go!" Ripper roared, seething with fury. "Fucking kill them all!" Crazed laughter spilled from his lips.

The doors of the clubhouse crashed open above us, and numerous Scorpions club members rushed out into the night. Gunfire erupted almost immediately. It wasn't hard to guess that the compound was under attack.

The Reapers were here. Was my Ace with them?

"They won't save you."

I dared to look into Ripper's eyes. "Even if I die, you'll never survive the night."

Above us, I heard the basement door fly open and bang against the wall. Footsteps hurried downstairs into the lower level. Would they stop my death in time?

Blood glistened on the wall from the beating I'd taken over the last few hours, and I blinked, hardly coherent. The fight was oozing out with my blood. I held onto consciousness, but barely.

Ripper grew furious, switching out his tools of torment again. He lifted the cat o' nine tails, ready to strike me again. I flinched as the lash tore at my ribcage, crying out as the last of my resistance crumbled. I wouldn't live through much more of this.

Toad appeared first, slamming his body into Ripper as the weapon knocked from his hand and fell to the ground. The two men ended up on the floor, pounding fists into one another. I tried to focus on my cousin, but I couldn't. The world was tilting on its axis, and I didn't think it would be long before I closed my eyes, never to open them again.

A shout of pure agony filled the stagnant air, and I knew who it was without looking.

My Ace.

"Davina!"

My head lifted, and through bleary eyes, I saw Grady.

"Fuck, baby," he cursed, whipping out a knife as he began slicing into the restraints. "I'm so sorry I didn't get here sooner. Fuck!" The serrated knife made short work of the bonds, and I began to fall forward, crashing into him. I didn't have an ounce of strength left.

His face twisted into a mask of outrage as Ace picked me up, holding me close against his chest.

"I've got you. I swear, my love. I'll get you to safety. It's going to be alright."

I tried to mumble a response, but I wasn't sure what came out.

"Hold still. I've got wrap you up. You're bleeding all over." His voice broke and I wanted to comfort him but I couldn't.

Gunfire was still loud upstairs. I could hear shouting, glass breaking, and the stomping of feet. Someone groaned as a bullet hit hard, and I noticed a biker clutching his abdomen. I hoped it wasn't any of the Royal Bastards.

As Ace rushed up the stairs, I could smell gasoline.

Shit!

This whole place was about ready to blow up!

Ace cursed, running outside as he held me tighter, rushing away from danger. The jostling wreaked havoc on my mind and body. I didn't know what was happening. Everything ached and burned, the material he used to wrap my body rubbing against all the raw and open wounds.

Moaning caught my attention as I realized I was the one making painful, whimpering sounds.

"Hold on a little longer. I've got you, Davina. Please, don't cry."

Was I crying? I couldn't tell. My hands refused to listen to my instruction or will and reach for my face to find out.

An enormous explosion rattled the air and shook the ground beneath our feet. Dark smoke flooded the sky as I looked up, catching the inky clouds rolling across the expanse.

"Grady," I whispered, spitting out the three words he needed to hear one more time. "I love you."

All I heard in response was his cry of horror. "Davina!"

"DON'T YOU FUCKING DIE on me, Davina," Ace ordered, his voice filled with agony. "I'm not letting you go."

My eyes fluttered as I opened them and turned my head, finding Ace in a chair next to me, his hands holding one of mine as tears lingered in his eyes. I couldn't wrap my head around that image of my strong, fearless Marine crumbling apart in front of me.

"No," I groaned, immediately snagging his attention. "Don't cry, babe."

He shook his head, lifting my hand to press a kiss on the surface. "You ghosted me. I can live with that but not with you running off and getting killed because you're too fucking stubborn."

"I didn't ghost you," I promised. "I never meant to leave you for long."

He stood, sitting on the mattress and scooting a little closer. His fingers gently caressed the side of my face, and I felt the bandage that covered most of my cheek. Shit. The knife.

"It's gonna leave a small scar."

"Won't I be a little sexier with it?" I joked as his sad blue eyes met mine.

"No," he growled, swallowing hard. "Fuck. Yes. That's not the point."

I sighed, taking a deep breath and releasing it. "I'm sorry, Grady."

"I know, precious." He leaned in, pressing a light kiss on the tip of my nose. "You own my fucking heart. You know that? The pain you're in, the suffering, it's fucking eating me alive. I want to go back and slaughter that motherfucker ten more times, each more gruesome than the last."

"Ripper is dead? From the explosion?"

"No, before it happened. Toad got his justice for all three of the people he loves."

Me. Blake. Laramie.

"It was worth it," I whispered, "to find him long enough for Ronin to find his attacker."

Ace growled again. "Fuck. You did that on purpose, didn't you? You fucking lured him in, knowing he'd hurt you so that Toad could find him."

"He's been waiting three years," I reminded Ace. "I couldn't take that kill from him, no matter how much I wanted to do it. So, I did the only thing I could. I detained Ripper long enough he couldn't escape justice anymore."

"I want to be pissed at you for that," Ace admitted, "but I can't."

"Say you forgive me," I pleaded. "I need you in my life."

"You've got me," he promised. "I love you, beautiful. It's as simple as that."

ROYAL BASTARDS MC

SIXTEEN

"YOU SURE ABOUT THIS? Ready to ride with us, you crazy fucker?"

Grim was a tough sonofabitch but I liked the way these men handled themselves. They weren't thugs, far from it. I'd watched Mercy's interaction with the Royal Bastards and I knew them to be loyal, fiercely protective of their own, and men of honor. They championed justice even if they weren't always on the same side as the law. The kind of brotherhood I shared when I served my country and the very thing I wanted to experience again. Nothing sweeter than knowing your teammate had your back.

Never thought I'd join a motorcycle club. Guess that was changing today.

Smirking, I nodded at my future pres. "Yeah. Let's do this."

Grim gestured to the open road and I followed, noting that most of the Royal Bastards brothers formed a long line behind us. We merged onto Hwy 95 in a long row of steel beasts, rumbling the earth as the desert flashed by on the left and right. Warm wind blew against my back and I relaxed, feeling a sense of belonging as profound as the bonds I knew in the fleet.

I wondered why we had to take this Devil's Ride.

Tradition? Necessity?

Who the fuck knew?

When we turned onto the desert, I didn't know what to say. Cactus and tumbleweed blew around us until we stopped far into the barren wasteland of the Great Basin. Somewhere, I heard a howl. Coyote?

I opened my mouth to ask Grim what was next when the scene before my eyes vanished and I stared into the crimson eyes of a hulking beast. Like an honest-to-fucking-God *monster*. Dark fur. Huge pointy teeth. Claws sharp enough to tear my body to shreds.

"Woah!" I shouted, falling to the side before I slammed onto the hot desert sand, not quick enough to prevent the ungraceful tumble. "Fuck!"

Dark horns protruded from the beast's skull as I blinked. *What the fuck?*

The massive monster snarled, blowing out air from his nostrils as it curled into vapors, rising up to mix with the clouds. A hissing sound escaped from blackened lips.

And then . . . *he disappeared.*

My mind couldn't grasp what was happening before a man took his place, staring at me with the same scarlet gaze that slowly faded into a shining silver. He wore a crisp dark suit with a blood red silk handkerchief poking out above his breastbone. Hair as black as midnight was slicked back as he grinned.

Oh, it wasn't anything normal or even fucking human. Shark-like teeth appeared in his maw, snapping slightly as our eyes met. I swear I saw a piece of flesh swiped away with his tongue.

"Grady Barnes," he greeted in a silken, seductive tone. "Hero. Badass Marine. Lover. Shall I go on?"

Okay, so he knew me. That wasn't the least bit terrifying or anything.

"No." I frowned, wondering what he wanted. Not a good idea to ask.

An amused chuckle shook loose. "You're taking the Devil's Ride. An audition, if you will."

"Audition?" For what? The Hunger Games? No, thanks. That shit didn't end well for anyone.

His grin widened. "To see if you've got what it takes to become a Reaper."

A Reaper?

"One of *my* Reapers," he emphasized like there were others that didn't belong to him.

Mouth gaping open, I tried to listen to his words.

"You should know me."

Something in my mind jostled the information free. Lucifer. The devil. The lord of Hell.

"Ah, yes. See? Not so hard."

"What do you want?" I asked, a little wary. The devil was a known trickster.

"Caution is good. Too much, though? A problem."

Right. Well, sorry. I didn't jump headfirst into shit. Not since I was a kid. "What's this about?"

Lucifer shrugged. "You want revenge?"

I shook my head. The man who hurt Davina died. I didn't care to waste my life on vengeance.

"Justice?"

Shit. That was a different subject.

"Yes, you do. What if I could promise that you would be able to destroy those who harm innocents? That you would rip their souls from their bodies and send them to hell for eternal punishment? Rapists? Human traffickers?"

The idea did appeal to me, oddly enough.

Lucifer shook out his hand and a contract appeared. "Sign it."

"What's the catch?" Like I wouldn't ask.

"Nothing. You send the souls I mark for destruction to me and you get to bond with the Reaper."

"That sounds too simple."

His eyes flashed red briefly before they faded into the same striking silver. "Oh, it is. But for you, I've got something special."

"What do you mean?"

"A bonus. Something none of the others have. A special gift for the ace."

Fuck. That didn't sound good at all.

But then I thought of Davina, and all the victims I couldn't help in the past, of all those assholes who hurt women and children, and I knew I made my choice as he chuckled. The parchment lined in gold appeared in front of my face and I lifted a hand, surprised when a slice appeared on my fingertip. Without hesitation, I signed my name, waiting for hellfire to swallow me up or some crazy shit.

I just sold my soul to the fucking devil.

Laughter bubbled out of Lucifer's mouth. "I'll be seeing you soon, Bones."

"Bones?" I asked, falling backward as I slammed onto the desert sand, landing on the ground a second time. Glancing up, I spotted the other Royal Bastards. All my new brothers.

Their eyes grew wide, each of them taking a step back.

"Oh, fuck," Rael blurted.

"The first of my kind," Lucifer's voice announced as we all shivered. *"The pale one. BONES!"*

I tried to grasp what he meant, staring at the others.

"What does Lucifer mean?"

Grim swallowed, shaking his head. "Well, Bones. You're a Reaper now."

"Just a little different than the rest of us," Wraith added.

"Why?" I asked, confused.

"Because you're solid fucking white," Diablo informed me. "Albino white from head to toe."

"Ain't seen nothin' like it," Bodie added.

My eyes widened and I cursed. "Well, fuck."

I knew there was a catch.

"YOU NEED A DRINK," Rael announced, strutting around the kitchen of my house like he goddamned owned the place, opening and shutting cabinets until he found my expensive whiskey. The fucker opened the bottle, too, not even bothering to ask. I shot him a glare as Diablo set up his equipment, snickering at my expression.

"Gonna take a few hours," Diablo began, "Get settled."

Sure, no problem. I wasn't anxious as fuck or anything after that visit from Lucifer.

"He's trippin', man," Wraith observed, pouring a shot of the liquor and handing it over.

"This shit never gets old," Rael agreed, opening a bag of popcorn and popping it into my microwave.

"Seriously?" I asked, gesturing to the mess he was makin' in my kitchen.

"What? This buggin' you?"

Fuck. I wasn't playing his game. Lifting a middle finger, I smirked. "I'm not that easy, princess."

Several of my brothers chuckled, and the noise soothed the restlessness I felt within. Something was off, and I couldn't quite figure out what the hell made my skin feel like a hundred insects were crawling all over it. I kept fidgeting, not noticing Diablo's frustration until he snatched the bottle of booze and shoved it in my hand.

"Drink. You're gettin' on my nerves. I've got to focus, or you'll end up with something fucked up on your skin instead of your Reaper."

Sighing, I gave a brief chin lift and tilted back the bottle, guzzling a few hefty swallows. The rich, honeyed taste melded with spice as it exploded across my tongue, and I finally relaxed. A few minutes later and I squinted at Grim. "Ready for that tattoo now, pres."

A dark chuckle fell from his lips. "That's good, Bones. Diablo already started."

Well, fuck.

"Where's Davina?" I slurred, looking around my kitchen. "Need my ol' lady."

"Not until I'm done," Diablo mumbled, shaking his head with humor. "You can fuck that feelin' out of your system later when I don't have a needle in your skin."

Feminine laughter echoed from my living room, and I realized my sexy goddess was close. Good. As soon as Diablo finished, I'd take her upstairs to ride my cock.

Rael munched on popcorn, spilling the shit all over my floor as I ignored him, focusing on remaining upright. My body kept tilting, and I wasn't sure if I imagined Diablo pushing me back up as I slumped over or not.

Exorcist lit up a smoke, and I mumbled under my breath about people abusing my house. Laughter followed my words as I tried not to concentrate on the pain. Diablo was a talented and skilled tattoo artist. I'd seen the ink my brothers had gotten. Shit was badass.

Sometime later, I heard pounding and wondered what was happening. My front door swung open as Lucky and Bodie stood shoulder to shoulder, blocking my view.

"Who's there?" I asked, squinting through my drunken stupor.

"It's fucking late."

I heard Twitchy scream as Diablo lifted the needle, cursing. My body moved so damn fast I hardly realized I was in the living room before I blinked, rushing to my ol' lady. Davina was in my arms, blubbering under her breath as she stared down at the body on the ground.

Sammy Cutter. My ex-girlfriend.

She was dead. My gaze swept over her mangled remains, noting that fresh bruises, cuts, and burns marked a large percentage of her petite frame. These wounds weren't inflicted when she was pushed from the van we chased down on Hwy 95. No. She survived that.

This was all new. Sammy had been tortured.

"That's the girl from the school," Davina correctly remembered. "She was with the Russians."

"Yes."

"The Russians hurt her and brought her body here. Why?"

Her gaze met mine, and I didn't lie. "Because of me."

"You know her?"

"Yeah, babe. She's my ex."

Her eyes widened. "You never mentioned it."

"It slipped my mind with all the other shit happening," I confessed. "We broke up over a year ago. I never expected to see her again."

Davina buried her head in my chest. "They did this to send a message."

"Same one they've been sending whenever we get in their way," Rael announced. "Fuckers want to intimidate us."

I looked to Grim. "You're already at war with them. Why kill Sammy?"

"To prove they watch us. You're one of us now, Bones. All Royal Bastards are the enemy to those cocksuckers."

Fuck. My goddess had a bright target painted on her back too. Suddenly pissed, I felt a stirring within, a dark presence that sent chills along my spine.

My body jolted as Davina backed up, staring at my face in awe.

"Holt shit, Ace."

My upper lip lifted in a snarl.

"Sorry. *Bones.*"

That was when I realized I wasn't alone and wouldn't be ever again. The Reaper. He was with me now.

I expected to feel uncertain or anxious, but I didn't. This felt *right*. Like everything I was missing up until now, all the shit I'd endured in my lifetime was all in preparation for the demonic entity now taking root in my soul.

Closing my eyes, I could sense each of the other Reapers in the room and even the ones still at the Crossroads.

My presence mingled with theirs, and we instantly bonded, recognizing kindred beings.

I'm a fuckin' Reaper. A Royal Bastard.

Wow.

It was real, and I never felt more ready to deal with the enemy.

"Their souls are fuckin' ours, brothers."

My voice. It wasn't normal. So deep, gravelly, and heavy.

"Damn, babe. You're smokin' hot," Davina gushed.

I turned, giving her a sly smile. "My ride or die."

"You bet your ass, Bones."

My Reaper sensed death, and his nostrils flared. Reluctantly pulling my gaze away, I stared at Sammy's body, feeling rage build underneath my skin. I almost vibrated with the intensity, whipping out my hand without conscious thought.

From my palm, a length of chain shot out, wrapping around her body and carefully tugging her closer. The Reaper understood she wasn't our enemy. My thoughts were his; his thoughts were mine. We shared emotions, desires, and needs.

My chest rose and fell, and I didn't know what to do about the young woman tragically murdered. I couldn't help feeling responsible for her death.

Shadow approached, his hand resting on my shoulder. "Bones? Let my shadows take her to the coroner. There's nothing we can do for her now."

My Reaper knew of the shadows that aided my brother. There was no threat, only assistance. The chains unwound from her remains and then whipped back, disappearing as I stared down at my hand.

"Well, that's new," Rael mused. "Spirit chains. Isn't that somethin', Bones?" He popped a handful of popcorn in his mouth. "Now that's entertainment."

I flipped him off as my Reaper growled. "Asshole."

Spirit chains? What in the actual fuck?

Davina placed her hand in mine, and I leaned down, capturing her mouth in a fiercely possessive kiss. Lust battled for control in my brain as I realized everything was more pronounced now—feelings, desires, fantasies. My groin ached with all the carnal thoughts dancing in my head.

Grim smacked a hand on my back as I felt his humor. He knew exactly where my thoughts had gone. The Reaper loved carnage, sex, and sin. He wanted more, lots more.

"Who dropped off the body?" I asked, finally focusing on the fact that someone had placed her on my porch, knocking on the door as the lot of us got drunk. The wild party must have prevented our Reapers from sensing danger, but that didn't make sense. I could feel everything, and I was fucking sober. That fast.

"We're gonna find out. Already sent Wraith and Exorcist."

I must have missed it. "I want to know details, pres. This is my goddamn home." Davina needed to be safe here because I wouldn't be intimidated by those fucking Russians.

"You'll get them." He ticked his head toward the kitchen. "Get back in the chair, Bones. Diablo needs to finish your tattoo."

Davina winked, swishing her ass as she walked upstairs. I'd be joining her soon. For now, I'd listen to my pres and get my ink.

But later, after my needs were met, I was going to compile all the info I had on these traffickers and deal out a little justice. After all, that was my new mission, and I never fucking failed.

EPILOGUE

"**F**UCK," I COMPLAINED, HITTING redial again.

Why the fuck wasn't Cindi answering her phone? The call kept going to voicemail, and it was driving me fucking crazy. With all the shit the club had gone through in recent months, I got anxious when she forgot to text. It was just a fucking spa appointment. Hair, nails, a little pampering.

Ever since she gave birth to our daughter, she didn't feel pretty anymore. I tried to tell my ol' lady that shit didn't matter six months after a kid popped out, but she didn't listen—stubborn woman.

So what did I do?

I bought her a certificate for the salon. Full treatment. All of the shit she loved.

Yeah, okay. I loved to spoil her. She deserved it.

Picking up my keys, I decided to drive over and see if her appointment ran late. Didn't take long since the business was only five minutes away. I pulled into a crowded lot since it was early afternoon. The place was busy as fuck. Scanning the vicinity, I didn't see her car.

Well, shit. She must have passed me on the way to the Crossroads. We missed one another.

Pulling out into the street, I made my way back home. Hit every single red light too. When I arrived . . . no Cindi.

Panic seized my chest. Where was she?

I didn't say a word as I caught a few of my brothers looking my way with concern. They lifted brows and a couple stood when I cursed, distraught with all the wild ideas floating around in my head. Pulling back on the throttle, I sped out into the street, heading toward Hwy 95.

"Fuck, babe. Where did you go?" I wondered aloud.

The wind snatched the words from my anxious chest as I swerved around vehicles on the road, desperate to find any trace of my woman. She wouldn't worry me like this. It wasn't like Cindi to take off without checking in first. Tension rippled along my shoulders. *Where the fuck was my ol' lady?*

Thirty minutes later, I found her car parked on the side of the road.

I pulled to a stop behind the SUV, jumping off as I ran to the driver's side. The doors were shut. No one was inside. No hint of blood or foul play. Not even her purse or phone.

My gaze lowered to the ground as I spotted footprints. Multiple sets. Among them was a dainty pair I recognized as Cindi's. Bike treads also left impressions in the sand as I squeezed my hands into fists. No biker from my club would do this. She didn't meet up with a brother.

Looking around, I found a path through the desert, leading into the unknown.

"I'm coming for you, Cin. I swear, I'll find you. If anyone hurt you, they'll meet my fucking Reaper."

I lifted my chin, settling my sunglasses over my eyes.

Time to let out my Reaper. He truly loved to hunt.

 Bones

"WHERE THE FUCK IS he?"

Shit. I knew that voice, and when Mercy was pissed, he roared like he was doing now.

Davina shrugged, snatching the popcorn bowl from Rael while she plopped down on one of the leather sofas in the common room.

Thanks, babe.

We both knew I was in some shit if her father hunted us down. Not that he had to go far. We spent a lot of our time at the Crossroads. As the newest member, I was getting to know my brothers and their quirks. Rael wasn't the only biker a bit strange in the bunch.

I held up my hands as Mercy stomped his way inside, immediately heading in my direction as he whipped off his sunglasses. "What's up, boss?"

"Like you don't fucking know," he spat, glancing briefly in his daughter's direction.

Davina didn't respond. A small smile lingered on her face as she watched the shitshow begin, still munching on popcorn as Rael tried to reach for the bowl, and she slapped his hand.

"I sent you to follow my daughter, not fuck her. Ace—"

Grim folded his arms across his chest, a smirk riding his features. "His name is Bones now."

Mercy glared, narrowing his eyes. "Like I give a fuck about that."

"My club. My members. My motherfuckin' rules, Mercy."

Mercy huffed a breath and pinched the bridge of his nose. "Fuck."

141

"I love her, Mercy," I responded in the quiet that followed. "You do with that what you want, but I'm in love with Davina, and I'm going to marry her," I announced with conviction.

Rael whistled low, grabbing a handful of popcorn.

Wraith smiled. Exorcist lit up a smoke, amusement visible as the flame danced over his features.

"You mean that?"

"Yes."

His shoulders relaxed, and he ticked his chin toward the bar. "Good. Grim, I need a fucking drink."

All 6'4" of his massive frame moved in that direction, gesturing for me to follow.

Once I had a shot of whiskey in my hand, he lifted his drink to toast. "Do anything to hurt my daughter, and I will fucking end you. Reaper or not."

I believed him even if my Reaper wanted to scoff. "I expect you would try." My lips twitched as he shook his head, pouring another shot.

"You protect her with your life. Love her, and we don't have no problems, *Grady*."

Mercy wasn't going to call me Bones, and I was alright with that.

"Daddy?"

He turned his head, blinking as sudden emotion flashed across his dark features. "Yeah, Davi?"

"I love you."

His empty hand clutched at his chest. "Love you more, baby. C'mere."

She rose off the couch, shoving the bowl of popcorn at Rael. Her eyes misted over, and I knew the relationship with her father would heal over time.

His big beefy arms wrapped around her as they hugged, each holding the other tightly.

"You love that Marine?"

"I do."

"Okay then."

The silence stretched between them, and I smiled.

Six hours later, I shut the door to our room, tossing my wallet and keys on the dresser. I'd gotten my own room right after my tattoo and the Devil's Ride. This was our sanctuary now until I could eliminate the threat against my woman.

Her eyes met mine as I turned, stalking my way over to the bed. Knee first, I leaned down and pressed her back against the mattress. "You happy, goddess?"

"Yeah, I am, Grady. With you and Bones."

My Reaper rumbled his approval as I reached for her wrists, pushing them above her head. I couldn't stop the movement of my hips as I rutted against her, revealing how much she turned me on. Didn't take much for my cock to grow excited around her, and now my Reaper was the same. Just as obsessed.

"Fuck me, Bones. I want to feel you both."

Both? Hell yeah!

A wicked grin twisted my lips. She wasn't getting any sleep tonight.

Thank you for reading!

This isn't the end, only the beginning. Look for more from Bones and Twitchy soon.

If you're new to the Tonopah, NV Royal Bastards MC, start here: *The Biker's Gift*

The next book in the series is about Lucky: *Haunting Chaos*

Twitchy appears in the following Royal Bastards MC books:

Grave Mistake

The Biker's Wish

Eternally Mine

Love motorcycle romance?

Check out these books by Nikki Landis

Ravage Riders MC

#1 Sins of the Father

#2 Sinners & Saints

#3 Sin's Betrayal

#4 TBD

Devil's Murder MC

#1 Crow

#2 Raven

#3 Hawk

#4 Talon

#5 TBD

Reaper's Vale MC

#1 Justified

#2 Stratified

#3 TBD

Lords of Wrath MC

#1 Tarek

#2 TBD

Iron Renegades MC

#1 Roulette Run

#2 Jester's Ride

#3 TBD

TONOPAH, NV CHAPTER

Pres/Founder – Grim "Grim Reaper"

VP/Founder – Mammoth

SGT at Arms – Rael "Azrael, Angel of Death"

Enforcer/Founder – Exorcist "Ex"

Enforcer – Jigsaw

Secretary – Wraith

Treasurer – Han "Hannibal"

Road Captain – Patriot (Marine)

Tail Gunner – Daniel "Lucky"

Founder – Papa

Member – Bodie

Member – Diablo (Cleaner)

Member – Xenon (Tech Spec.)

Member – Bones

Member – Shadow

Member – Toad

Prospect – Spook

SNEAK PEEK CROW

Hot, BONE-DRY AIR swept across the back of my neck as I rolled to a stop, the front tire of my hog resting ahead of the faded white line painted on the asphalt road. I paused at the intersection, obeying the order to stop at a red light though there wasn't much point. The hour was late, and if I hadn't already had a few beers and several shots, I probably would have blown right through the red light without a second thought. But now, legally drunk but not feeling any of the pleasant side effects of the liquor, I gripped the handlebars with my gloved hands and waited impatiently for the light to change.

There was no traffic, hardly even more than a few rolling tumbleweed to keep my ass company. I rode into town after nearly four hours on the open road, but this wasn't a scenic tour on my bike. Riding back into Vegas wasn't something I had ever intended to do again, and if it wasn't fucking important, I wouldn't be here. You could bet on that.

That was why I stopped at the bar outside of town and proceeded to drink as much as the sweet little blonde bartender would give me until closing. Probably would have taken her home and offered her a ride she wouldn't forget if I weren't so fucking torn up inside.

Alcohol and sex only masked the problem anyway. The issue was my reason for returning to The Roost. My chest constricted as I thought of my father and all the shit of the last five years.

Fuck.

I scrubbed a hand over my face and closed my eyes briefly, opening them again as I caught the headlights in my mirror, taunting me as they'd done the day I left.

It was too dark to see the make and model of the cage, but I didn't need to see to know Sheriff Taylor watched, his car idling on the road as if he dared me to turn around and face him. Didn't matter what that asshole thought. I wasn't a kid he could push around anymore.

The traffic signal swayed in a gust of wind as it switched to green, and I lifted one hand, leaving only my middle finger exposed.

Fuck off, Sheriff Taylor.

A dark chuckle left my lips as I sped across the intersection, my bike rumbling with a low, deep-throated vibration as I passed the closed shops and through the barren streets. Even Vegas had an hour or two when it shut down. Prostitutes and gamblers all had to sleep at some point. Of course, I was only on the outskirts of the city now. The strip never went silent. Flashing neon lights, the jangly music, and the whir of spinning reels accompanied by loud beeps and the chimes of slot machines, drunken revelry, and the lure of sex were only a few of the enticements that bombarded every visitor in the city of sin.

My destination led me in another direction. A place I avoided for as long as possible but could no longer put off. That tight feeling in my chest grew until I nearly choked on the lump that rose, lodging in the center of my throat. The gates of Palm Northwest Mortuary & Cemetery loomed ahead as I approached, parking in the empty lot as I glided to an unceremonious stop.

I stood, stretching my legs and back, gazing at the perfectly landscaped grounds of the lot. My eyes roamed over the palm trees, weeping willow, tulip poplar, sycamore trees, Nevada's state plant sagebrush, and other blooms that offered pops of color in the moonlight, thriving in the sandy, dry climate. If it weren't for the city lights, I could have enjoyed the starry night sky, but I knew if I rode out to Tonopah, I'd be able to see them for miles without anything in the way or obscuring the view. Maybe I'd visit Grim and the Royal Bastards soon and check in on the club. Knew quite a few of those rowdy fuckers, and it had been some time since I'd seen them.

A watery oasis surrounded by various rocks that included limestone, sandstone, and shale glittered like diamonds as gentle waves rippled the surface a short distance ahead. Grass and sand competed for dominance along the grounds, but the lawn was obviously mowed often and maintained well. Hell, it was fucking green in the summer. That said a hell of a lot, considering how hot and dry the desert was this time of year.

Fountains, numerous gardens, and other unique memorial art spanned the entire forty acres of land. Grass-level headstones of granite and bronze were organized in innumerable rows by the water.

I strolled toward the fence and hopped over it, heading in the direction of the Freedom Garden. A tribute to veterans, this part of the cemetery honored military service men and women from all branches and their dedication and sacrifice to our country. I caught the flag billowing in the breeze and felt a twinge of emotion. My old man didn't want me to follow in his footsteps or those of my grandfather, who served in the Vietnam War.

I never understood when I was a teen. Words like sacrifice and honor were concepts that I was only beginning to fathom. It would take another ten years before I matured enough to forgive my overbearing father for his mistakes. Such was the naivety and foolishness of youth. Now, it was too late to speak words that would never be heard.

As I trudged along the pathway in my boots, my steps were confident, only stopping when I arrived at the correct grave, marked by a single upright headstone in black granite. A Harley was engraved into the surface by laser, memorializing the final wishes of Austin Derek Holmes Sr. Everyone knew him as Rook, the president of the Devil's Murder MC. I knew him as something much more intimate.

"Hey, pops," I choked out, staring down at the space his body occupied, the smooth, freshly mown surface hiding the powerful, intimidating man I'd grown up calling father. "Bet you didn't think I'd be back here so soon."

The wind lightly whistled through the nearby trees, and I heard a rustling among the leaves, a slight flapping of feathered wings that accompanied the melodic sound.

"Raven ratted you out, old man. He told me about that conversation you had a week before you died. The one where you told your V.P. what you wanted in case shit went south."

Lowering to a squat, I plucked the pocketknife from inside my cut and held it, my grip tightening as I mulled over my next words.

"I wasn't here when you needed me." My teeth clamped down as my jaw locked, and I had to force a breath through my lungs. "I'm fucking sorry I let you down. I should have had your six that day. Maybe if I had been here, I could have prevented your death. I'll always wonder if being with you would have made a difference or if those bastards would have killed me too."

Without fanfare, I yanked the leather glove on my left hand off, shoving it into the back pocket of my jeans. I flicked the knife open and sliced the sharp blade across my palm, forming a fist as dark droplets of blood seeped through the cracks in my fingers and dripped onto the grass below.

"I swear to you that I will find the assholes responsible for your death, and I will fucking end them. I won't rest until every motherfucker involved pays for killing the president of the Devil's Murder MC."

My hand lifted, and I kissed my bloody fist, then pulled out a bandana and wrapped it around the wound, hardly noticing the sting.

"I'll avenge you," I whispered, standing to my full height, squaring my shoulders back as I felt something light drop onto my right shoulder, tiny talons gripping the leather of my cut. The weight shifted slightly and then settled, a single raspy *caw* bursting from the beak of the bird I called a friend.

My uninjured hand reached into my pocket, dug around for a penny, and then placed the coin on the cool, smooth surface of the headstone. Nickels and dimes created a long row down the length, proving the men who served with my father honored his memory. Spinning on my heel, I faced emptiness of a future without my father and his gruff, loyal, steadfast leadership.

I'll make those motherfuckers regret they ever heard the name of the Devil's Murder MC.

Beady eyes stared from all directions as I noticed the crows crowding the branches of nearby trees. A few hopped along the grass. Several of the birds landed on the headstones of neighboring graves, but not a single crow touched my father's final resting place. Dozens of the creatures had silently invaded the cemetery without ever making their presence known. Not that I wasn't aware. They were only an extension of my body, like a limb with its own separate conscious thought.

Onyx feathers glistened like an oily stain blotting out the moon as more crows arrived. Each bird perched on the edge of its spot, keenly aware of every movement in the vicinity, even the wind. Expectancy hung heavily in the air as a few birds grew vocal, and *caw caw...caw caw* echoed in a regular pattern. The chatter increased before I ticked my head toward the sky, and the murder flew upward in unison, flooding the darkness as I headed toward my bike.

Black wings speckled the sky in a pulsing, rippling glide that spanned far enough to block out the twinkling stars and shy, hazy crescent moon. The murder followed closely as I straddled my bike, fired up the engine, and sped away from the cemetery with one destination in mind.

It was time I returned home.

Crow was ready to roost.

CROW, Devil's Murder MC is now available!

One Hell of a ride!

Royal Bastards MC Facebook Group -
https://www.facebook.com/groups/royalbastardsmc/

Website- https://www.royalbastardsmc.com/

ABOUT THE AUTHOR

DARK. WICKED. ROMANCE.

Nikki Landis is the USA Today & International Bestselling, Multi-Award-Winning Author of over 50 romance novels in the MC, reverse harem, paranormal, dystopian, and science fiction genres. Her books feature deadly reapers, dark alpha heroes, protective shifters, and seductive vampires along with the feisty, independent women they love. There's heart-throbbing action on every page as well as fated mates and soul bonds deep enough to fulfill every desire.

Made in the USA
Coppell, TX
29 August 2022

82273172R00102